Also by the author:

Haunted Bones, (poetry)

Dirty Little Angels

Chris Tusa

Livingston Press
The University of West Alabama

Typesetting and page layout: Joe Taylor
Proofreading: Margaret Walburn, Shelly Huth, Stevi Bolen, Asa Griggs,
Terry Kennedy, Connie James, Allie Ellis, Katherine Tracy,
Joseph Abraham, Emily Mills, Ivory Robinson, Jennifer Brown
Cover design and layout: Jennifer Brown
Cover Photo: Heather Loper Walker

Part of this novel appeared (in a slightly different form) in *StorySouth*.

Acknowledgments

Thanks to BJ and Jesse for all the free therapy sessions, for all the inspirational meals, and more importantly, for being so damn interesting. Thanks to Ferma for teaching me about life, and for being the best friend a boy could have. Thanks to Michael Garriga for putting aside your own writing to read countless drafts of this manuscript. Thanks to my wife for being perfect in every possible way. Finally, thanks to my mother, father, and stepfather for always encouraging me to follow my dreams.

Livingston Press is part of The University of West Alabama,
and thereby has non-profit status.
Donations are tax-deductible:
brothers and sisters, we need 'em.

first edition
6 5 4 3 3 2 1

for Pamela

Dirty Little Angels

Chapter One

The baby was a white fist of flesh. Mama had placed the ultrasound photo atop her dresser in a sterling silver frame. That night, when the pain bent her over in the kitchen, I imagined that same white fist punching her insides black-and-blue. When Daddy called from the hospital to tell us she'd lost the baby, my brother Cyrus said I shouldn't worry. He said the baby didn't feel any pain, that at nine weeks it wasn't anything but a ball of meat squirming in Mama's stomach. He said it hadn't even sprouted arms or legs yet, that it still had a fish brain and gills growing in its neck.

That night, I dreamed of Mama's flesh creaking as the doctor unstitched the trapdoor in her stomach. Her insides looked like crushed red velvet, and the baby's skin was blue as a robin's egg. I imagined the stitches in her stomach, tiny black mouths puckering between the folds of her belly. I remember wondering where the baby's cries had gone, if they had stayed inside Mama's body after the doctors stitched the trapdoor shut.

Nearly six months later, I was sitting in front of Ben Franklin High in my yellow flower dress, studying for my science test, thinking about the baby again, my fingers tracing the pink gills of a fish in my biology textbook. As I stared at the fish, I heard the crackle of gravel and what sounded like the faint moan of a car horn. I looked over my shoulder and saw a rusted blue Hyundai with a dented fender idling in the parking lot behind me. It was my brother Cyrus.

As I walked up to the car, Cyrus revved the engine. The inside of the car smelled like bug spray. Ever since I could remember, Cyrus had always been a hypochondriac. He was always reading some medical encyclopedia, convinced he had suddenly come down with some dreadful disease. A few weeks back, he'd seen some story on the news about the West Nile Virus, and ever since then he'd been spraying himself down with bug spray before he left the house.

As I climbed into the passenger's side, he turned up the car stereo, and Mystikal's "Tarantula" crackled through the speakers. I closed the door and buckled my seat belt, and Cyrus rammed the car into drive and spun the tires, until a cloud of brown dust swallowed the car.

Cyrus was wearing a New Orleans Hornets jersey and a black Reebok skullcap. He had a thin line of brown hair for a beard, and he'd shaved little lines into his eyebrows. Two years ago, Daddy had helped him buy the old Hyundai from a junk yard in Independence. He'd spent the whole summer souping it up. It had red racing stripes, bald, rotten tires and silver spoked rims. He'd covered the seats with leopard-skin seat covers, and he had a mini eight-ball hanging from the rearview mirror.

"You going to Verma's?" Cyrus asked.

"Yep. Why didn't Daddy pick me up?"

"He's down at the pool hall." Cyrus took a drag and blew the smoke out his nose. "Man stays down there much longer, they gonna start charging him rent."

Since before I was born, Daddy had worked down at the meat packing company on Julia Street as an Assistant Supervisor, that is, until last December, when he'd gotten laid off. For the last few months, he'd been collecting unemployment checks. He spent most days down at Spider's Pool Hall nursing cocktails or at the Fair Grounds betting on horses.

"Hey, can you give me a ride to Meridian's tomorrow?"

"Not tomorrow." Cyrus took two quick drags and flicked the

Lucky Strike into the wind. "Gotta go downtown and meet my parole officer."

Cyrus had been arrested three times, once for stealing chrome rims from a warehouse in New Orleans East, and another time for snatching car stereos from the parking lot of the gun show. This time, he'd got caught selling a quarter bag of weed to a boy over on Almonaster Street. Mama agreed to bail him out, but only if he promised to join the church and get saved. Mama said Cyrus'ss soul was blacker than mud, and that only the preacher's water could raise up his dead soul. Cyrus agreed to get saved. Mama and I even went down to the church that day to watch Brother Icks dunk Cyrus in the baptismal pool. When I asked Cyrus what it was like, he said it felt more like being drowned than being saved. Mama was convinced that the water had cleansed his soul, though, because two days after he was saved, Cyrus went down to Ink Dreams and had a line from *Revelation* tattooed on his biceps that said: "He Shall Rule Them with an Iron Rod." Wherever he went, he kept a pair of brass knuckles in his back pocket. On Saturday nights, he and his friends rode up and down Paris Road in their rickety cars looking for boys to fight. Other nights, they hung out in an old abandoned bank down on Elysian Fields.

"So," I asked Cyrus. "When are you going to take me down to the old bank with you?"

"You're too young to go down there."

I grabbed my lipstick from my purse and pulled down the visor mirror. "Meridian wants to go too," I told him, puckering in the mirror as I spoke. "She thinks you're cute." I knew Cyrus had the hots for Meridian. He always said she had hips that could make a glass eye wink. I'd even found a picture of Meridian in his wallet one time. He'd actually cut out her picture from the Ben Franklin Yearbook and stuck it in his wallet like some kind of creepy stalker or something.

Cyrus grinned as he pulled into the parking lot of Verma's apartment complex. "I'll think about it." He put the Hyundai in neutral, and I climbed out. As he pulled off, I noticed Verma in her pink robe, in the courtyard of the apartment complex, sitting in a lawn chair near the edge of a green swimming pool, smiling. She was a skinny black woman with mossy gray hair, and she had a gold tooth with a star etched into it. Glaucoma had swallowed her right eye in a filmy white shroud, and diabetes had eaten up the veins in her feet. Mama and Daddy had known Verma for years, and I'd known her practically all my life. Since before I was born, she'd lived in the same ratty apartment complex on Pelopidas Street. Most days, after school, I went to her apartment to help her wash clothes, dishes, whatever she needed, really. Every day, before I left, she gave me a five dollar bill that smelled like perfume.

"Where's that brother of yours off to?"

"I think he's going back to work," I said. "Then down to The Lakefront for the races."

"Has the devil burrowed into that boy's skull?" Verma wheezed, a glass of Pepsi sweating at her feet. "If he don't watch it, he's gonna end up like that boy with the paper bag face."

Verma had worked for a woman whose son's Dodge Neon fishtailed through a field while racing down at the Lakefront. She said the gas tank on the Neon had burst into flames, that the boy had been swallowed in an orange ring of fire, and that after the accident, when she visited the boy in the hospital, his face looked like a brown paper bag with two holes ripped out for eyes.

"Where's your momma? Over at the house?"

"Don't know. Think she's cooking dinner." Mama wasn't cooking dinner. She hadn't cooked dinner one time since the miscarriage. Daddy said she was dead to the world.

"What about your daddy?"

"He's down at the pool hall."

"Already?" she asked, pressing the glass of Pepsi against her forehead as she spoke. "He come home last night?"

"I don't think so."

"I'm gonna have to have a talk with that father of yours again," she said, rattling the glass of Pepsi. "Somebody needs to light a fire under that man's ass. He's been outta work for almost three months now."

"I think it's been more like five."

Verma reached into her robe pocket for a Chesterfield. As she lit the cigarette, I motioned to her for a drag. "What you want a cigarette for, Hailey? So you can get hooked like me? You too young to start killing yourself."

I motioned to her again and she handed the Chesterfield to me. "All right, dammit. Just one quick one though. And make it fast. Your momma and daddy gonna skin me alive they see me sneaking you drags."

I sucked the smoke deep into my lungs.

"Your Uncle Errol been by the house again?" Verma asked.

"Yep." I handed the Chesterfield back to her. "He came by Thursday."

"Old rotten-toothed slug." Verma scratched an itch deep in the clump of her grey hair, took a drag off her Chesterfield. "He still on your daddy to sell the house, huh?" She flicked her ashes into a folded paper napkin in her lap and took another drag. The tip of the cigarette glowed bright orange. "Well, don't go worrying yourself over it, Hailey. That sneaky-ass uncle of yours ain't gonna get his grimy hands on your momma and daddy's house. Not if I got anything to say about it."

A few years back, Verma had gotten an insurance settlement from Sears after she'd slipped and broken her hip while shopping there. Daddy said she had more money than the Pope, and he couldn't believe that with all the money she had, she still lived in the same ratty apartment complex. Mama said it was because Verma actually saved her money, rather than living off credit cards and pay-day loans like most people he knew. Daddy even suggested that we borrow money from Verma, but Mama wouldn't have it.

"I got a friend," Verma said, "down at Wal-Mart. Says he can get your daddy a job."

"Really? Doing what?"

"It ain't nothing special. Just a cashier job. But it'll tide y'all over. Till your daddy can get back on his feet."

"I hate to say it, but I doubt he'll go."

"I'll dress your daddy up and haul his ass down there myself if I have to."

Verma took another drag off her cigarette and snuffed it out with her green slipper. I helped her out of the lawn chair and we went inside.

For the rest of the afternoon, I helped her stuff artichokes and peel shrimp for stew. Before I left, she gave me a five dollar bill. The word "five" had been colored green with a ball point pen, and Lincoln's eyes had been cut out.

*   *   *

When I got home, I was surprised to notice that Mama's Saturn was gone. The yard was littered with Daddy's clothes, jeans and work shirts, shoes like empty mouths. A pair of his leather gloves was dangling from the branches of the crepe myrtle. They were brand new, still stitched at the wrists, and they looked like two black hands joined in some kind of upside-down prayer.

When I got inside, I could hear Mama calling to me from her room.

"Hailey? That you? Would you make me some tea? And could you get me an aspirin for my head?"

I boiled some water for tea. When it was done, I headed toward her room, grabbing an aspirin bottle from the bathroom cabinet on the way.

Mama's room was dark, and she was buried to her neck in a white afghan, her face glowing in the blue light of the television. Daddy's side of the bed was empty. A few weeks back, he'd started sleeping on the sofa. Mama said he snored too loud, and that when he was in bed with her, she couldn't get any sleep. I told her about those nose strips that all the football players wear, but she said nothing ever worked the way it was supposed to. I'd seen Daddy sleeping a thousand times, and I'd never heard him snore. Not once.

As I walked into the room, I noticed the framed certificate Mama had gotten for being Nurse of the Year. It said, "To Lena Trosclair, LPN, in Recognition of Your Outstanding Work." The only pictures in the room were the ultrasound of the dead baby on Mama's dresser and two paintings of Jesus, one of him hanging on a cross, staring down with those terrible blue eyes, a golden halo atop his head, and another of him holding up his left hand, a bright crimson heart glowing in his chest. There were no photographs of me, no pictures of me holding an ice cream cone, chocolate dripping down my arm. Not one of me in my purple dress, the purple ribbon Verma gave me fluttering in my hair.

Only Jesus and the dead baby. In my family, it was as if you had to be dead to get noticed.

Mama was chubby with a bun of yellow hair. Her arms looked like two white loaves of bread, and she had a crooked nose planted between two round cheeks that looked like perfect scoops of mashed potatoes. When I got to her bed, I put the cup of tea on the nightstand, opened the aspirin bottle, and pulled the cotton ball out. Mama opened her mouth and closed her eyes, and I placed the aspirin on her tongue. "What's wrong?" I asked, handing her the cup of tea.

She brought the cup to her lips, blowing on the tea as she spoke. "The finance company came by and took my Saturn today. Said your daddy was late on the payments again, so they took it."

"Is that why Daddy's clothes are all over the lawn?"

"Do you know how humiliating that is? Having some stranger drive up and take your car 'cause you're too broke to pay the bill?" Mama took a sip of tea. "I had to wait two years for your father to get that promotion before I could get that car. Finally, I get one, and look what happens."

"I'm sure he can get you another car."

"You know how long it'll take before he can afford another car like that?"

Mama had come from a wealthy family, and when her and Daddy decided to get married, against my grandma's wishes, Grandma disowned her and cut her out of the will. Ever since I could remember, Daddy had always worked overtime at the meat packing company, trying to make enough money to buy Mama all the stuff she wanted, but for some reason, Mama always seemed to act like the money he made was never enough.

"Anyway, it's not just the car. Your Uncle Errol keeps coming around, looking for his money. Says if we don't pay, he's gonna take the house. Hell, we can barely even pay the bills with all the loans we got. I even had to stop getting those massages I was getting. Course, your daddy thinks they're some kind of luxury, but the doctor told me himself that weekly massages are important, especially if you want your back to heal properly."

A few months before she'd gotten pregnant, Mama had thrown her back out moving a patient from one bed to another while working a graveyard shift at Mercy Hospital. Daddy said it was hard to believe that someone could throw their back out just from moving a patient from one bed to another. Mama said Daddy didn't have a clue how difficult being a nurse was.

"I just wish I could go back to work. All I do now is sit up in this bed and rot." Mama put the cup of tea on the nightstand and grabbed a nail file from the top drawer. "And when I'm not worrying about money, all I'm thinking about is that dead baby. I keep praying," she said, filing the nail on her pinkie until the white tip was a perfect half moon. "Hoping God'll come along and save us from all this mess."

Sometimes, at night, I'd hear Mama saying her prayers, asking God to save our family, asking him to watch over me and Cyrus and Daddy. I'd even tried to pray a few times myself. I'd get on my knees and cup my hands, waiting to hear God's voice roll over me like a black wave, but nothing ever happened. I wanted him to save our family the way he'd saved other families, but every time I got on my knees and spoke to him, it seemed like no one was listening.

Since Mama couldn't sleep, we decided to watch TV for a while. On the news there was a story about a talking fish. The newscaster said a 20-pound carp in New York that was packed in ice suddenly flipped out of a delivery crate and started speaking in Hebrew, shouting all these apocalyptic warnings, saying he was the soul of some preacher who'd died a few days before. The people they interviewed claimed it was a miracle, and that the talking fish was proof that God really did exist. I laughed at first, because the story reminded me of that *Sopranos* episode when Pussy got reincarnated into a fish. But as we watched the newscaster interview some lady with big hoop earrings, I started to hope that God would send me some kind of sign, that somehow he'd fly down to Earth and perform some miracle that would cure my whole family.

*   *   *

That night, the moon looked like Verma's cataract, and the sky, black and cluttered with clouds, was crying little drops of rain. Around two a.m., I woke to the sound of Daddy's Nova growling down the rutted clam-shell driveway. I could hear his keys jingling in his pocket as he walked along the porch, the splintered floorboards creaking beneath him. As I fell asleep, I listened to the rain-filled gutter outside my window, the slow drip of water like a wristwatch ticking in my ear.

Chapter Two

For the last few months, I'd noticed that sometimes my thoughts would get scrambled, so much that the thoughts themselves felt like roaches crawling around in my head. It had all started after the miscarriage, after Mama and Daddy started talking about getting a divorce. Ever since the baby had died, Mama and Daddy hadn't spoken to each other as much, and when they did, it was like they were staring through each other, as if they didn't recognize each other anymore.

The roaches were crawling in my head again, so I decided to skip school. I sat in my room for a while and read. I looked up mental disorders on the Internet. It showed schizophrenia and depression, and it said that people's mental states were controlled by electrical currents in their brain. I wondered if the wires in my brain were broken, like the brains I saw on the Internet.

*   *   *

That night, Cyrus and I picked up Meridian and headed down to the old bank. Cyrus had agreed to bring me to meet his friends, as long as I brought Meridian. The old bank was on Elysian Fields, between the EZ

Check Cashing building and an old run-down crack house. The large, glass drive-up window of the old bank had been spray-painted black, and some of the letters of the name "Gentilly Commerce Bank and Trust" had fallen down. The T was missing so that the word TRUST now spelled RUST, and a large black letter C dangled from the side of the building like a broken halo.

Cyrus said his friend Moses Watkins was renting the place, and that he was planning on making it some kind of drive-through church, but it still looked like a bank to me. The lobby was empty, except for a few lawn chairs and a stained mattress with rusted springs sticking out the side. The walls were covered with posters, mostly of half-naked girls in string bikinis, rappers with muscles carved into their chests sporting gold chains and fists full of money. Across the room, a girl in a pink half-shirt was passed out on the mattress, a half-drunk bottle of Purple Haze in her hand.

Moses was sitting in the corner in a green lawn chair, a tin can of sardines in his lap. He was a wiry black man with a pot belly, and he had one gold tooth surrounded by a row of yellow teeth, and a large afro with a blue comb sticking out the side. His eyes were tiny and round, like drill holes in a casket, and he was wearing a black and yellow 8 Ball jacket with the arms cut off and black jeans with missing knees. I'd heard that he'd been hit by a car while crossing St. Anthony Street a few years back. The rumor must have been true because he had a thick purple scar the shape of a question mark on his head where his afro wouldn't grow.

After Cyrus introduced me to Moses, he and Meridian wandered over to the corner of the room, where a few other kids were shooting dice. Moses introduced himself and grabbed a lawn chair that was leaning against the cracked, yellow wall. I asked him how long he'd lived in New Orleans, and he said that he'd come here a few years back, after working as a preacher and as a Ferris wheel operator for a traveling carnival. He said he'd started working for the carnival just after he'd been released from Angola Prison, and that since he didn't have any preacher skills, he stole most of his sermons from a man named Billy Sunday. He said that Billy Sunday was a famous evangelical preacher who used to travel the country spreading Jesus' word. Moses's favorite Billy Sunday saying was about sin. He'd said he was against sin, that he'd kick it as long as he had a foot, that he'd fight it as long as he had a fist, that he'd butt it as long as he had a head, that he'd bite it as long as he had a tooth. And when he was old and fistless and footless and toothless, he'd gum it till he went home to Glory. Moses said he must have preached those words a thousand times. When I asked him if anybody ever found out that he was using another preacher's sermon, he just smiled, picking a piece of sardine from his dirty teeth. He said that all the people really wanted was Jesus, and that every night he served Jesus up, like a pretty little leg of lamb, for the sinners to sink their teeth into.

He told me about how he was planning to turn the bank into a drive-through church, that he'd gotten the idea while he was in prison, and that with work and raising kids, people just didn't have time to go to church anymore. He thought a drive-through church would be a good idea, and he said that once he got the place cleaned up, he planned to open it up to the public every Sunday and use the bank's drive-up window to hand out a weekly scripture. He said if people wanted a hamburger and fries, they could drive right up to a window and get it, and that salvation shouldn't be any different. He even talked about eventually sending scriptures as text messages directly to people's cell phones.

After we finished talking, I hung out with Cyrus and the other boys for a while. From talking them, you'd think Moses was a celebrity. Most of them seemed obsessed with his violent past. Rumor had it that Moses had killed a man while he was in Angola, and it seemed like the boys were attracted to this, as if they somehow got a rush from hanging around someone with a reputation for being dangerous. Most of the boys worshipped the rappers they watched on TV, and to them, Moses was just an older version of Ludacris or Fifty Cent. They also seemed to like the fact that Moses had connections with a bunch of local drug dealers. They even said that Moses got them free drugs whenever they wanted, and that a few weeks back, Moses had brought them a whole batch of acid. Cyrus said it was the coolest acid he'd ever seen, and that each hit had a little red cross on it.

Later, when we were leaving, Moses walked us out. His car was parked next to Cyrus's. It was a ratty green Omni with bald whitewalls and a broken taillight. It had yellow racing stripes, silver hubcaps, and diamond studded mud flaps. The driver's side fender was dented, caked with grey Bondo, and the windshield was a spider web of cracks, coated with white clumps of bird shit. SATAN SUCKS was spelled out across the back window in gold letters, and a yellow bumper sticker read: IF GOD DIDN'T WANT US TO EAT ANIMALS, HE WOULDN'T HAVE MADE THEM OUT OF MEAT.

On the dashboard was a statue of Mary clutching a bright red heart. In the backseat was a black and white pitbull with a spiked collar around his neck. He had a dry red scab on his head and a scar that curved around his nose. As I looked through the window at him, he opened his mouth, panting at me with his big pink tongue. A silver tag was dangling from the collar. It said HITLER.

When we got to Cyrus's car, Moses told Cyrus they needed to get some statues to make the bank look religious. Moses pulled the blue comb from his afro and began yanking it through the black hairs of his mustache. "When I'm done," he smiled. "The place'll look like a goddamn cathedral."

Chapter Three

The Dead Goat was a cluster of old, abandoned warehouses off Jefferson Highway where lots of high school kids hung out. At some point, the owners had left it to rot, and over the years people had started dumping trash there. The whole area was littered with gutted cars, piles of junked boards, clumps of concrete and drywall, even the rusted skeletons of old washing machines and refrigerators. Originally, the area had been called Cold Storage Road, but people started calling it The Dead Goat after the police got a phone call one Halloween that a group of Satan worshipers had done a sacrifice there. Rumor had it, the police found a pentagram of gasoline burning in one of the warehouses and a dead goat dangling from a telephone pole. The goat had been gutted, and its eyes had been plucked out.

Meridian and I had gone to The Dead Goat to meet our friend Jay. Me, Meridian, and Jay were in tenth grade at Ben Franklin High. Jay was a skinny kid with a bleach blonde flat-top, a hair lip, and a tattoo of a flaming fleur-de-lis on his right biceps. He'd brought his cousin Chase Haydel with him, an older-looking guy with slick black hair that looked like it had been painted onto his skull. He looked like he'd rubbed tanning cream all over his body because his skin was the color of candied yams. He had a small red mouth that looked like a doll's mouth, and his eyes were the color of a hearse. You could tell he was older by the way he dressed. He was wearing Oakley sunglasses, a blue silk shirt and white pants. With the dark skin and the silky clothes, he reminded you of Al Pacino in *Scarface*, without the Cuban drawl and the machine gun, of course. Jay said that Chase had gone to school at Holy Cross, but that he'd dropped out in the tenth grade. He'd been to jail twice, once for beating up a boy at the A&P and another time for smashing the windshield of his girlfriend's pink Corvette with a lead pipe.

As I sat on the dented hood of Meridian's father's Buick, I watched Meridian pull a lipstick from her purse. Like me, she'd spent her whole life in New Orleans, and her family was as crazy and lopsided as mine. Maybe that's why I liked hanging out with her. At first glance, she was the kind of girl whose eyes you wanted to scratch out. But over time she grew on you, like a tumor, like a bloody scab you didn't dare pick at.

"Here," Meridian said, smiling with her fat collagen lips as she handed the tube of lipstick to Chase. "Put your number where I won't lose it." She had a noose of dirty blonde hair dangling down her back, and her Calvins were cut so low you could see the top of the purple thong she was wearing. She climbed onto the Buick, leaned back on the hood and lifted her blouse until you could see the edge of her black lace bra, the silver skull and crossbones pendant that hung from her waist chain flickering in the sun.

A few months back, Meridian's dad had taken out a Pay Day loan to buy her a boob job. I watched Chase's eyes drift over Meridian's boobs. They were obviously fake, but Chase didn't seem to care. I watched him circle a chocolate brown mole on her hipbone with the number zero, watched him draw a red number three that curved around her bellybutton. As he did this, he glanced over at me.

"Your brother ain't Cyrus Trosclair, by chance, is he?"

"Yep, that's my brother," I said, sitting up.

"He hangs out down at the old bank with Moses Watkins and them, right?"

"Yep."

"Man, he's a legend." Chase smiled at me.

Meridian grabbed the lipstick from Chase and stuck it in the back pocket of her Calvins. "You got a cigarette for me?" she asked, her sandled feet dangling, the black polish on her toenails chipped away.

Chase took a drag from his cigarette, pulled a pack of Pall Malls from his shirt pocket and handed one to Meridian.

Jay grabbed a bottle of Zima from the six pack at his feet and unscrewed the cap. "How'd you two do on that algebra test?"

"Thibodeaux's a witch," Meridian wheezed, her voice like the soft swarm of bees. "She never even covered that crap in class."

"You see her husband?" Jay asked, wiping a drop of beer from his hair lip. "At the pep rally, I mean?"

"He was there?" I asked. "Which one was he?"

"The one in the dark blue suit with the yellow tie," Jay said. "With the black hair. And the glasses."

"The *retard* that followed her around like a dog the whole time," Meridian snapped. She took a drag off the cigarette and rolled her eyes. "Woman makes me wanna puke."

"Man." Chase glanced over at Meridian, his mouth twisted into a smile. "You must really have it in for this woman, huh?"

"Meridian's got it in for everybody," Jay said, smiling as he took a swig of beer. "Her daddy calls her the Black Plague on Two Legs, says instead of blood, she's got septic water running though her veins."

Meridian glared at Jay as if she wanted to strangle him with the purple Victoria's Secret thong she had on. "Shut up, you walking miscarriage. Shouldn't you be at work by now anyhow?"

"Shit," Jay yelled. "Shit. Shit. I gotta go, Chase. Right now." Jay tossed the Zima bottle into a patch of weeds. "I mean it. I gotta go."

"Jesus Christ, Jay." Chase hissed. "I just opened my goddamn beer."

"I mean it. If I'm late again, Lois is gonna fire my ass."

Chase flashed a pissed-off look at Jay, then walked over to Meridian and took the cigarette from between her fingers. He took a drag, blew the smoke out the corner of his mouth. "So tell me, Meridian. What's a girl like you looking for in a guy?"

Meridian smiled with those fake collagen lips of hers. "Me? I like the dumb, slab-of-meat, brain-dead kind." She fondled the tail of his shirt, looking up at Chase as she spoke. "The kind so muscle-heavy they might just suffocate me when they pin me down."

Chase smiled back at her. "Well shit . . . we're a match made in Heaven." He took another drag off the cigarette and handed it back to Meridian. "Don't you forget to call me now."

Chase and Jay walked over to the weedy edge of the canal where Chase's car was parked. It was fully-restored, black 1968 Firebird with silver mag rims. He had a silver fish emblem on his rear fender, like the one you see on all the Christians' cars, except this fish had legs.

"Nice, huh?" Meridian asked me.

"Yeah. He's yummy."

"I'm talking about the car, Hailey." Meridian took a drag, bit her lip, then blew the smoke out the corner of her mouth. "He's ugly as dirt," she smirked. "Gotta nice ass, though." She took another drag and smiled. "Maybe I could teach him to walk backwards."

I laughed and took the cigarette from Meridian, staring at it before I took a drag. There was a long grey curled ash on the end, and a red ring of lipstick around the filter where Meridian had slobbered all over it.

As Chase pulled off, Meridian was staring at a blackbird perched on the hood of a rusted Cadillac. It looked like a black flag fluttering in the wind. Meridian raised her right hand as if it were a gun, took a drag from her cigarette and pointed the tip of her finger at the blackbird, her left eye squinted. I leaned back on the hood of the Buick as sunlight ricocheted off heaps of sheet metal.

*　　*　　*

That night, I went with Cyrus and Moses to Krispy Kreme. While we were eating, Cyrus saw this kid named Seth Connors who'd jumped him a few years back. Seth had moved away after senior year, and nobody had seen him since then. Cyrus told Moses the whole story, and Moses said we needed to teach him a lesson.

When Seth was done eating, we followed him out to his car. I rode with Moses, while Moses and Cyrus followed Seth to wherever he was going. On the way, I told Moses how Mama had prayed to God, hoping he'd save our family, how for some reason, God had never answered her prayers. He said that sometimes people had to suffer before they could be saved. He told me about his father, how when Moses was little, his daddy used to ask him questions about the Bible. Moses said that if he didn't answer a question correctly, his father would beat him with an extension cord. He even showed me some of the scars on his back where his father had beaten him. They looked like black worms slithering under his skin.

We followed Seth for twenty minutes, all the way to Fat City. By the time we pulled into the parking lot of Seth's apartment complex, it was starting to rain, and the air was black, as if all the stars had fallen out of the sky. Moses pulled in behind Seth and killed the engine. By the time Seth got out of his car, Cyrus was walking toward him. Seth was wearing a Black Sabbath shirt, and he had a carton of Camels under his arm. He smiled when he saw Cyrus, his mouth like a red scab, his long wiry hair tucked behind his ear. "Didn't I kick your ass already, Eminem?"

Cyrus smiled back at him, and before he even knew it, Cyrus had socked him in the face with his pair of brass knuckles. As Seth stumbled to his knees, Moses stepped out of the Omni and walked over to him, rubbing an apple against his shirt, a switchblade flickering in his other hand. He cut a piece of apple, holding the sliver of apple against the blade of the knife with his thumb as he brought it to his mouth, sucking the piece of apple from the blade, then tossing what was left of the apple into a muddy ditch, his eyes like fireflies blinking in a clump of dead weeds. He stepped toward Seth, grabbed him by the hair and put the knife to Seth's throat. "You ready to get saved, Boy?" Moses hissed, but Seth didn't answer. He punched Seth in the ribs, then Cyrus moved in, socking him in the gut with the brass knuckles. As Cyrus slugged Seth in the stomach, Moses kicked him in the ribs. In a twisted way, it was kind of exciting, knowing that the boy had jumped Cyrus a few years back, and that he'd finally gotten what he deserved.

When Seth finally stopped moving, Moses and Cyrus scurried back to their cars. Moses climbed into the Omni, breathing hard. He cranked the engine and turned the car around, then followed Cyrus back to Orleans Parish.

*   *   *

When we got back to the bank, Cyrus and Moses smoked a joint and talked for a while. Later, on the way home, Cyrus stopped off at the Circle K for a can of potted meat. I told him I was worried that Mama and Daddy might get a divorce, and that sometimes my thoughts got so scattered they felt like roaches crawling around in my head.

He said he thought it was normal to feel like that from time to time, and that he didn't know what to do when Mama and Daddy started talking about divorcing each other. He said for a while he felt depressed, like he had a hole in his heart and his insides were empty, but that after a while the depression turned into anger. He said he used to get Daddy's punching bag out of the garage and sock it for hours, but that after a while he got tired of socking the bag, and that soon he started to wanna sock a real person. I told him that was probably why he liked fighting so much, and that even though I usually thought fighting was stupid, I felt like Seth deserved what he'd got. I laughed under my breath, telling him how Mama would've probably asked him to pray for Seth rather than sock him.

"She's such a damn hypocrite," he said, licking pink bits of potted meat off his finger. "I swear, it's like she went to the bathroom one day to have a bowel movement, and when she came back, she'd suddenly found religion." He scooped a pink lump of potted meat from the can with his finger. "Anyway, even if she did believe in all the crap she's always ramming down our throats, what's the point? She spent the last six months throwing money in the tithe jar every Sunday, waiting for some angel to land on her shoulder and cure the whole family. And where's it gotten her?"

"So you don't believe all the stuff she's always talking about? That Jesus is coming back? To save you from your sins?"

"To tell you the truth, I'm not even sure he exists. And even if he did exist, why would he wanna come back? He already flew down to Earth once. And look how much good that did him. Don't get me wrong, I like reading the Bible. And I love the stories, especially in the Old Testament. God didn't take any shit back then. He'd turn your ass into a pile of red dust if you didn't do what he said, strike you dead with a lightning bolt. But as far as God and Jesus being real? I dunno. They just never seemed like believable characters to me."

"Why'd you get saved? Just because Mama wanted you to?"

"Yeah. I guess. I figured if getting baptized'll get her off my back, then so be it."

"You didn't feel anything when they baptized you?"

"Whatcha mean?"

"I dunno. Mama claims you can feel the spirit washing over you when you get baptized. You didn't feel anything?"

"Nope." Cyrus pulled a pack of Lucky Strikes from his shirt pocket and shook one from the pack, speaking out the side of his mouth as he lit it. "Unless you count that stupid preacher's fingernails digging into my neck as he dunked me."

"So you're an atheist?"

"I dunno. I thought about being an atheist, but the whole idea of somebody's *belief* being that they don't *believe* in anything doesn't make much sense."

"You could always be an agnostic."

"What do they believe?"

"My history teacher said it comes from the word *knowledge* in Greek, and that *Agnostic* means 'no knowledge.' Basically, agnostics think that human beings don't have enough knowledge to know the answers."

"Sounds like a fancy word for dumbass to me. I don't mind not knowing for sure, but I don't wanna be some kind of dumbass."

I laughed. "What about Judaism?"

"I don't think I'd like being a Jew. It seems like someone's always out to kill you. First Jesus, then that whole mess with Hitler. I think I'd feel like I was walking around with a bull's eye on my back all the time."

"Yeah, but that's no reason to avoid a whole religion. Anyway, my teacher says every religious group gets persecuted at some time or another. He says it's part of being religious."

"Thanks, but I think I've had enough persecution for one life."

A few minutes later, Cyrus turned up "Cupid's Chokehold" by Gym Class Heroes on the CD Player. I watched him smiling, tapping the steering wheel to the beat of the music, all the while thinking of

Chase, imagining his little red doll's mouth, his candied yam skin, as I stared out the car window, stars blinking through black walls of pine, the silver breeze crawling through my hair.

Chapter Four

When I woke up Sunday afternoon, Daddy was standing outside in the yard shoveling a mound of black dirt. He was planting a batch of black-eyed Susans around the crepe myrtle in the corner of the yard, his t-shirt a circle of sweat, a hose coiled like a blacksnake at his feet. I decided to watch TV for a while. There was this documentary on CNN about this archaeologist who'd found a caveman in a block of ice. As I watched the scientists chip away at the ice, I thought about how the world around me had become fuzzy and scattered, how for the last six months or so I'd felt just like that caveman must have felt, as if I'd been staring at my life from behind a blurry pane of glass as the world passed me by.

At some point during the documentary, I heard a car outside. When I peeked through the drapes, I saw a shiny yellow Hummer. It was my Uncle Errol. When Daddy saw the Hummer, he leaned his shovel against the crepe myrtle, and Uncle Errol killed the engine and got out of the car.

Uncle Errol was thin with murky brown eyes. His face had been stuck with so many Botox treatments, it looked like a mask. He'd gotten a botched hair transplant a few years back, so his hairline looked like a doll's, a perfect row of tiny black holes with thick black hairs sprouting out.

The house we lived in was the same house Mama had grown up in. But since Grandma cut Mama out of her will, and since she'd left all her money to my Uncle Errol after she'd died, the house was officially Uncle Errol's. Luckily, Uncle Errol had never tried to take the house, but over the last few months, Daddy had started missing the mortgage payments, so every now and then Uncle Errol would drop by, like a cancer that kept coming back, pressuring Daddy to pay up or sell. I'd never really liked Uncle Errol, mostly because he always seemed like he was rubbing his money in Daddy's face, waltzing around in those shiny, worm-colored slacks, a silver cell phone headset screwed onto his skull, a new Bluetooth Blackberry chirping in his pocket.

As I walked onto the porch, the screen door creaked and Daddy looked up.

"Hey, Chickadee. You hungry?" He wiped the sweat from his eyes. "Lemme talk with your uncle for a minute and we'll go to Nacho Mama's and get some food."

I sat on the steps and waited for Daddy to finish talking to Uncle Errol, knowing full-well why Uncle Errol had stopped by.

"Guess you know what I'm here for?" Uncle Errol said, staring at Daddy through the shiny mirrors of his sunglasses.

"I told you Errol. I don't have it."

"It's been three months, Jules." Uncle Errol pulled a silk handkerchief from his pocket and put his foot on the rusty bumper of Daddy's orange Nova. "You not leaving me much choice." He spit into the handkerchief and began shining one of his black patent leather shoes. "I got a business to run, you know that. What you doing with those unemployment checks you get every month?"

"Light bill, phone bill, credit card bills. I'm up to my eyes in goddamn bills, Errol."

Uncle Errol spit into the handkerchief again. "Shep said he saw you down at the track on Sunday."

"You know how that is. Urgent situations call for urgent measures."

"Yeah, well. You better find some way to hustle up the money. And fast." Uncle Errol grinned through the shiny mask of his face as he put the handkerchief back in his pocket and then climbed into his Hummer. "You got one more month, Jules. Or else I'm gonna have to take legal action."

As I listened to Uncle Errol and Daddy talk, I started to worry that we might lose our house. I remembered what Moses had told me, that sometimes people had to suffer before they could be saved. Maybe this was why God hadn't saved my family. Maybe my family had to suffer before it could be saved. This is what I thought about on the way to Nacho Mama's.

*   *   *

Nacho Mama's was a tiny little Mexican restaurant a few blocks from my house. The sign outside had a large red pepper with a huge black mustache wearing a purple sombrero. The inside of the restaurant was dark with little candles on each table. Daddy and I sat in a booth near the window.

Our waitress, Iris, like all the other waitresses there, was wearing a skimpy little Mexican skirt and a white blouse tied in a knot just above her belly-button. She had freckled skin, dyed red hair, a fake black mole on her cheek, and a plastic yellow rose stuck behind her ear. If you looked close, you could see a batch of zits on her forehead that she'd covered up with makeup.

"Hey Jules," she said. "You decided to come back for more, huh?" While she spoke, she stared at the black shark tattoo swimming on Daddy's shoulder blade. "You haven't had enough of me yet?"

Daddy grinned. "I'm here for tamales, Iris."

"I got tamales," she smirked, chewing on a cracked red fingernail.

Daddy pulled out his nicotine inhaler and took a puff. "Heard you got yourself a roommate, huh?" he asked, sucking a puff of nicotine deep into his lungs, his mouth the perfect shape of an O.

"Yep. That warthog girlfriend of Bookie's moved in."

"Cherice? When she move in?"

"It's been about two weeks, I guess. Girl sits around the house all day, hogging up all the bath water, shoveling through bags of chips with those frying pan hands of hers. Not to mention sunbathing on the patio. Spends half the morning in the bathroom greasing herself up like a sausage."

"Cherice?" Daddy laughed. "You've got to be kidding."

"Nope. Every morning she shoehorns that fat ass of hers into this pathetic little polka dot bikini. Then she takes to strutting around the patio out front. You got to see this bikini, Jules. Every God-forsaken fiber of that thing struggling to keep that woman's nightmare-of-a-body from full view. It's enough to throw the apartment complex clean into therapy."

"How often does she sunbathe?"

"Every day. When the sun's got the courage to come out, that is. Hell, just this morning I woke up and looked out the window, you know, hoping to catch a glimpse of a blackbird or a butterfly or something, and like a damn cancer, there she was, as if Death had gone and dressed itself in spots and parked itself on my front lawn. I can't even stomach going outside anymore. Went out in the yard Saturday to plant some tulips, and there she was again," Iris said, adjusting the fake rose behind her ear. "Spent what coulda been a perfectly fine Saturday watching obesity have a picnic on my front lawn."

Iris yapped on like that for almost twenty minutes, telling Daddy about all the latest gossip at the apartment complex where she lived. Daddy ordered tamales, a fish taco, and black bean soup, and I got a crab meat enchilada and an order of sopapillas. When we were done, Daddy asked me if I wanted to go to Spider's and shoot a game of pool. As we were leaving, he planted a kiss on the waitress' cheek, right above her fake, black mole.

*   *   *

Spider's Pool Hall was at the end of Elysian Fields. It was a pink building surrounded by a patch of dead grass, and the front of the building was cluttered with engine blocks and chrome rims.

When we got inside, I ordered Daddy a Bloody Mary while he grabbed a table. A few minutes later, I found him on the back corner table racking the balls. A skinny man with long tangled hair was staring into a smudged mirror, picking at his dirty teeth with a toothpick. There was a fat man next to him dressed in overalls leaning against the jukebox eating a pickled egg.

"They were at the Fair Grounds in New Orleans," the skinny man said, pointing the toothpick at Daddy.

Daddy rubbed his hands together in a white cloud of chalk. "Nah," he argued. "It was the dog races in Mobile. I heard it straight from Dove's mouth." Daddy took a sip from the Bloody Mary and the piece of celery almost poked him in the eye. "Dove said Errol swung at the kid first. Said that boy was the biggest, meanest boy he'd ever seen. Said he had a chest like a damn accordion. Arms like ham hocks. Said Errol told that boy he was gonna split his lip, spill those gold teeth of his all over the floor. Unfortunately, for Errol, that's not what happened. Turns out, in one quick lick, that boy balled up his fist and socked Errol with all he had. Punched the smile clean outta his head."

Daddy squinted and leaned over a rainbow of pool balls. "Must have knocked his vision loose too, 'cause Dove said Errol's eyes went North and South like his thoughts were crooked, like his brain was squirming in his head." He squinted again and tapped the cue ball with the tip of his stick. He banked the nine ball off the one, and the nine hit the corner rail. "Then, right when Errol's arms went drunk, that kid leaned in and laid another one square in his gut. Bent Errol over like he was praying."

As Daddy walked back to the table, he glanced over his shoulder and winked at me. He leaned his pool stick against the jukebox and walked over, the Bloody Mary in his hand. He bent down and planted a kiss on my forehead, and when he did, the glass tilted in his hand and red drops of Bloody Mary juice sprinkled my knee. "I need my good stick if I'm gonna beat these wise asses," he said. "Whatcha say, Chickadee? Wanna go home and get it for Daddy?"

*   *   *

Our house was only a few blocks from the pool hall, so Daddy let me take the Nova. He'd let me drive it from time to time, mostly when he was too drunk to drive. As I drove down Elysian Fields, I thought about what Moses had told me, how sometimes, when God didn't answer your prayers, you had to take matters into your own hands. I knew Daddy kept a fresh pint of vodka in the glove compartment, next to a loaded pistol he'd won on a bet. So, when I got home, I got this bright idea to pour some of the vodka out and replace the rest with water. Daddy was so drunk half the time, I was sure he wouldn't even notice.

Once I'd finished watering down the vodka, I went over to the garage and opened the latch on the shed. Whenever Daddy stayed at the pool hall too long, Mama hid his pool stick on him, and most times, she hid it in the shed. The shed was cluttered with stacks of books and boxes of clothes. I looked around for Daddy's pool stick, but I didn't see it anywhere. Toward the back, I saw a large black trunk wedged between a mattress and a blue bicycle. It was long and slender like a coffin, and the top was chipped and peeling, caked with dust and rat droppings. I wiped the lid off and popped open the latch with a screwdriver. Inside, I found stacks of construction paper—mostly cards I'd made for Mama when I was in middle school. At the bottom, I found a Christmas tree angel with a bent halo, a black comb with three missing teeth, and a Cabbage Patch doll with one eye. I even found a drawing I'd made for Mama while I was in Ms. Scully's third grade class. In the picture, Mama was standing under an orange sky, her fingers were mangled, and her mouth was a crack growing beneath her nose. Two dimples opened like holes in her cheeks, and her eyes were X's. A pink ear dangled from her chin, her smile was crooked, and her arms were waving in the wind. She looked like she was drowning.

In the opposite corner of the shed, I could see what looked like a white tarp draped over some boxes. I stepped over a pile of cinder blocks, and under the tarp I found a pile of small white statues stacked on top of each other. It reminded me of the pictures I'd seen from the Holocaust. There was a statue of a nun with a missing right hand, a little girl with fat cheeks and wings sprouting from her back, and a boy bent on one knee clutching a rosary. While I stared at the rosary in the little boy's hand, I noticed a silver flicker in the reflection of an aquarium, and as I glanced over my shoulder, I saw Cyrus standing in the doorway.

"Nice, huh?" he said.

I covered the statues with the tarp and turned around. "Yeah." I told him, my voice cracking.

"Moses wanted me to get some statues for that drive-through church he's been talking about." Cyrus took a drag off his cigarette. "Whatcha doing in here?"

"I'm looking for Daddy's pool stick. Mama hid it on him again."

"He's down at the pool hall again?"

"Yeah. He sent me home to get his lucky stick."

Cyrus sighed. "It's amazing how lazy that man is. You know Verma got him an interview down at Wal-Mart the other day?"

"Yeah. She told me she might be able to get him a cashier job."

"Yeah, well, he didn't even show up." Cyrus swatted a fly from his nose. "The way he ducks outta every opportunity he gets, you'd think success was a guillotine looking to land on his neck."

Stepping over the stack of cinder blocks, I began to make my way toward the shed door, until Cyrus's voice stopped me.

"Fix the edge," he said, his smoky words drifting in the air.

"What?"

"The edge." He snuffed the cigarette out against a rusted screen door that was propped against the wall. "Of the tarp."

The nun's left hand was sticking out from under the tarp. I tugged on the edge so that it covered her fingers. When I was done, I stepped over the stack of boxes until I'd made my way back to the doorway of the shed. When I got there, Cyrus reached behind a stack of fishing poles, pulled out Daddy's pool stick, and handed it to me.

As I locked the shed, Cyrus walked over to his Hyundai, climbed in, and started revving the engine. He backed the car up and swerved onto a patch of dirt surrounding the swingset and yelled to me from across the yard. "Tell Mama I'm going to the Voodoo game. I'll be back later tonight." He put the car in drive and spun the tires, as I stood there in the yard, the heat snaking up my legs as the Hyundai and the red sky behind it disappeared in a white cloud of dust.

Chapter Five

By the time I got back to Spider's with Daddy's stick, it was almost six o'clock, and the sky looked like Mama's black sequined dress. Daddy was on the back table shooting a game of nine-ball. He'd won the first three games off some fat man with a bad comb-over. The man had that seen-a-ghost look when Daddy slammed the nine in the corner.

While Daddy played pool, I sat at the bar drinking Shirley Temples and talking to Yvette the bartender, a skinny woman with blonde hair and brown leathery skin. Yvette looked like she hadn't dyed her hair in months because she had black roots growing out of her skull. Daddy had told me she was a meth addict and that she'd gone to jail one time when the police caught her shooting up behind some building on Chef Menteur Highway. She had tiny yellow bruises all over her arms and neck and a little red sore on her lip.

"Your Momma back at work yet?" Yvette asked, combing a hand through her dirty hair. She dropped a cherry into a glass of 7-UP and handed it to me.

"Not yet," I said. "Her back's still giving her trouble."

"It's hard to work," Yvette said. "When you're in pain like that."

"Yeah. The doctor said she could have surgery, but I think she's scared."

"I don't blame her. Surgery's dangerous. My stepfather went under the knife for his back. 'Bout two years ago, I guess, and he still ain't recovered. Not really." As Yvette was talking, I glanced over my shoulder and saw someone standing behind me. It was Chase.

"Hey, Yvette?" he said, smiling. "Can I get a Purple Haze?"

Yvette reached under the bar and handed the beer to Chase.

"Hailey, right?" he asked, turning his eyes on me. He pulled out a sweaty wad of money from the pocket of his white slacks, licking his fingers as he counted off three wrinkled dollar bills. "Meridian's friend, right? I'm Chase. Remember? We met down at The Dead Goat a few days back."

"Oh yeah," I said, as if I barely remembered him.

"You here by yourself?"

"Nope. Just waiting for my daddy to finish playing pool." I could feel Chase's tiny black eyes resting on my chest.

"Nice dress," he said, taking a swig of his beer.

I rolled my eyes. "Shouldn't you be painting Meridian's toenails or something?"

Chase smiled and took another sip. "You don't like me too much, do you?"

"Just sick of watching guys drool all over Meridian, that's all. It gets pretty damn old after a while." I picked through the bowl of pretzels, glancing up at Chase between words. "You know, she thinks Iraq's in Mexico."

"What?"

"Iraq," I said, chewing on a pretzel. "On a test, Meridian put down that it was in Mexico. She actually thinks it's a city near Mexico. A city for Christ's sake."

"Holy shit," Chase smiled. "You mean to tell me Iraq's not a city in Mexico?"

"You can joke all you want," I said. "All I'm saying is she's a few clowns short of a circus, that's all."

"Yeah, well. Dumb girls are underrated."

"Oh really?" I grabbed a pretzel from the bowl and bit off a piece.

"Yeah. I love dumb girls, specially, the real dumb ones. Hell, my last girlfriend was dumber than a box of hair, and I dated her for almost two years. Being dumb's not a crime. Hell, there's far worse things than being dumb."

"Like what?"

"Well, for starters you could be armless."

"Armless?"

"Yeah. You know, you coulda been born without arms. Hell, there's plenty babies born without arms."

"Plenty, huh?" I said, sucking the salt off my fingers.

Chase put his hands behind his back. "Whatcha think? Would you still think I was cute? If I didn't have any arms?"

"Who said I think you're cute?" I smiled and grabbed another pretzel from the bowl. "So, what else would be worse? Than being dumb, I mean? Besides being armless?"

"Let's see. You could have leprosy."

"Who the Hell gets leprosy these days?"

"Plenty people get leprosy. As a matter of fact, there's a leper colony right here in Louisiana. In Carville. Maybe I could take you there. Sightseeing sometime."

"I don't think so."

"Why not? You got something against lepers?"

"Is that what you call entertainment? Going to see a bunch of lepers?"

"I dunno. I guess I just find shit like that interesting. Anyway, it's not much different from some of the crap on TV these days."

As Chase took a swig of Purple Haze, I imagined some bizarre version of *Big Brother,* a bunch of lepers locked away in some loft apartment to compete against one another for brand new SUV's and trips to Bermuda. I smiled, imagining the druggy leper forming an alliance with the sorority girl leper, the night vision camera spying on the slutty leper as she sneaked from room to room, the Christian leper thumping her Bible, trying to convince the lesbian leper that all homosexuals burn in Hell.

"Sorry," I said, "but I don't find people with diseases entertaining."

"Did you know in the 1600's there was this lunatic asylum in London called Bedlam where they actually charged people admission to watch the mental patients? They actually considered it entertainment."

"Really?"

"Yep. It's probably only a matter of time before they start charging admission at Carville too. What do you say?" Chase laid his hand on my knee, and I have to admit, I kinda liked it. "You wanna go with me? While it's still free to get in?"

"I don't think so." I took a sip of my Shirley Temple and smiled. I saw Daddy motioning to me from across the bar. "I think my daddy's ready to leave. I'll see you around."

Chase winked. "You can bank on it."

* * *

On the way home, Daddy asked me if I'd stop off at the Circle K. He told me to roll up the window and to stay in the Nova. I watched him wander over to the strip club next to the Circle K, then I rolled the window down. He stood there for a moment looking at his watch, until a minute or so later when a woman walked out in a long trench coat. It was Iris, the waitress from Nacho Mama's. I killed the engine, and since there wasn't much traffic on Chef Menteur, I could hear what they were saying.

"I'm sick of your excuses, Jules," she said.

Daddy was balancing himself against a handrail with one hand, the other hand gripping his nicotine inhaler. "I'm just saying, Iris." He combed a hand through the last few yellow strands of hair left on his tiny pink head. "There's a right time for everything. This just isn't the right time."

"There's no proper time to leave somebody, Jules." She was speaking out the side of her mouth as she lit a cigarette. "You either leave or you don't. That's it."

"I have a family, Iris," Daddy told her. "What kind of person would I be if I left my family?"

"Family?" Iris told him. "What do you think I got, Jules? For Christ's sake, Garrett's up at Mercy Hospital, lying on his deathbed." The dry air must have been creeping up her legs because she closed her coat. You could see that all she had on under that coat was a black bra and a pink thong.

Daddy didn't say a word. He was staring down at the ground.

Iris rolled her eyes. "I gotta get back to work. I've only had this job a week, and I sure as Hell can't afford to lose it."

"I hate you working in a place like this."

"Whatcha mean, a place like this?"

"You know, a place that objectifies women."

Iris laughed. "Maybe I like being objectified. You ever think of that? Anyway, someone's gotta pay the bills, Jules. If I got to be objectified in order to pay the rent, then so be it."

"I'd sure like to objectify you right now."

Iris smiled. "I gotta go, Jules." She took a final quick drag off the cigarette, tossed it in the dirt and mashed it with the pink toe of her pump. I watched her walk down the gravel path that led to the front door of the strip club. When she got to the doorway, she turned and watched Daddy stumble back to the car.

I thought long and hard about leaving Daddy in that parking lot. It made me so mad to know that while Mama was rotting in bed every night, Daddy had been gallivanting around town with some silly waitress from a Mexican restaurant. When he got back into the car, I didn't say anything at first. I pulled out of the parking lot and headed down Chef Menteur. As we pulled up to a red light, Daddy turned on the radio.

"You know," I said, turning the radio off. "I heard you back there."

He was staring out the car window, at a long-legged woman in a black leather skirt pumping gas. "Heard what, Chickadee?" he asked, sucking on his nicotine inhaler.

"I heard you," I said, "talking to that lady back there. At the strip club."

He glanced up at me, sucking on the inhaler, his eyelids like two little cracks in his face. "What lady?"

"That Iris lady. The one you were flirting with at Nacho Mama's. What were you doing talking to her, anyway?"

A smirk squirmed in the corner of Daddy's mouth. "Nothing good."

I kept one hand on the steering wheel and reached my other hand across the seat, slapping Daddy on the shoulder as hard as I could while I tried to steer.

"What the Hell are you doing, Hailey?" he yelled, his bird's nest of yellow hair dangling in his eyes.

I slapped him one final time on the back of his head, leaned back into my seat, grabbed the steering wheel with both hands and squeezed it until I could see the blue veins bulging in my wrists.

"Jesus Christ! Are you trying to kill me?"

"Someone needs to beat some sense into you. Staying at Spider's to all hours of the night. Bringing your own daughter to a strip club in the middle of the night to go see some woman you're running around with? I mean really, Daddy. What the Hell's wrong with you?"

"I think I'm manic depressive."

"Would you stop being so damn dramatic."

"I'm serious." Daddy grabbed the nicotine inhaler from between his legs and took a puff, glancing out the window at a junkyard cluttered with clumps of gutted cars. "I think I've got some kind of chemical imbalance or something."

"Is that why you didn't show up for that job interview? Because you have a chemical imbalance?"

"What job interview?"

"Cyrus said Verma got you a job interview down at Wal-Mart. He said you didn't even show up."

"Come on, Hailey. Do you really expect me to work at Wal-Mart?"

"What's wrong with Wal-Mart?"

"Do you know how much money I was making at the meat packing company? You really think a job at Wal-Mart's gonna pay all the bills we got? Not to mention, all your mother's shopping sprees and massages? Anyway, Wal-Mart doesn't even give their employees a lunch break. Didn't you see that special on Dateline? Some Wal-Mart over in Florida stuck a retarded boy out in the Garden Center and made him lug around carts of flowers all day in the hot sun."

"Mentally challenged." I said.

"What?"

"You're supposed to call retarded people mentally challenged now."

"Fine," he said. "Mentally challenged then. Either way, they worked that poor kid like a goddamn mule until he finally came down with a heat stroke. They even refused to pay his doctor's bills. I can't work for a place that treats people like that. Hell, I might be broke but I haven't lost my ethics."

"You don't seem to have any problem ignoring your ethics when it comes to marriage."

"I love your mother, Hailey. You know that." Daddy didn't say anything for a moment. "Guess your Grandmonster was right, huh? She told your mother I'd never amount to anything."

"Grandma wasn't right, Daddy."

He rubbed his forehead with a pink hand, glancing out the car window again, at a dark wall of pine trees lining the highway. "My life's a wreck, Hailey. I turned out just like she said I'd turn out."

"Mama told me about what Grandma did when you two got married. The way she treated you, how she cut Mama out of the will just for marrying you, how she never even came to see Cyrus in the hospital when he was born. It wasn't your fault. If it was anybody's fault, it was Grandma's fault."

"Come on, Hailey, if it wasn't for me, your momma wouldn't have any of these money problems. She'd be rich. Hell, you'd be rich too."

"I don't care about being rich."

"Yeah, well, maybe you don't, but your mother sure does."

As I came to the intersection, Daddy raised a pink hand to his mouth and shut his eyes tight. "Can you pull over, Honey? I think I'm about to puke."

I pulled the car over, into what looked like a gravel driveway leading to a row of storage buildings, and Daddy opened the car door, leaned his head out, and spit into the dirt. When he was done, he closed the door and wiped his mouth with the sleeve of his shirt, then glanced out the window, the inhaler clenched between his teeth, his eyes rolled toward a pale moon hanging outside the car window.

After that, we didn't say anything the rest of the way home. When we got to the house, I walked Daddy to the couch. Mama was already asleep. I tucked him in and kissed him on the cheek. When I got into my room, I found a box of hair dye on my bed. The day before, I'd asked

Mama to get it for me at the grocery store. After I finished highlighting my hair, I looked up Mercy Hospital in the Yellow Pages. I knew Iris's last name was Guidry, and I remembered that she'd referred to her husband as Garrett when she was talking to Daddy. I called the hospital, and sure enough he was registered there. I wanted to visit him and tell him what his wife was doing behind his back, tell him that she was sneaking around with my Daddy while he was rusting away in that bed. The next day I planned to ask Meridian if she'd drive me over to the hospital.

That night, for some reason, I dreamed I was in a hospital, strapped to a gurney, surrounded by doctors. I was drifting above myself, as if I had died. My skull was cracked open and light was pouring from my head.

Chapter Six

On Monday, when I got to school, I found Meridian in the parking lot, sitting on the hood of her father's black Buick. For some reason, I couldn't get Chase out of my head. I knew Meridian liked him, but I didn't care. On my way to school, I'd sat in the back of the bus, writing Chase's name on the inside of my chemistry notebook, imagining his veiny hands, his candied yam skin, his voice warm on my neck, my name ripening in his little red doll's mouth.

As I got closer, I realized Meridian was talking to Chase. She was telling him the story of the beauty pageant she'd won in third grade. I'd heard the same stupid story a million times. Listening to it again, I swear I could almost feel the chunks of black bile churning in my stomach.

"They squeezed your feet into these little stinking heels," Meridian said, fingering her silver waist chain as she spoke. "Eight years old, and they got you strutting around on pumps. We looked like a bunch of goddamn china dolls on stilts. Then, they plaster your face with makeup. It was a goddamn circus, lemme tell ya."

Chase was drinking a Zima, his eyes stuck on Meridian's stomach. "So, did you win?" He wiped his mouth with the sleeve of his shirt.

Meridian reached into the black mouth of her purse and pulled out a tube of pink lip gloss. "Of course I won," she said, circling her lips with the lip gloss. She put the lip gloss back in her purse, then reached over and ran her finger along the lip of the bottle. "You shoulda seen those little runts squealing their guts out, Baby. Every one of those rotten little bitches wanted that tiara."

As her hand crept across Chase's muscled chest, Meridian glanced over at me. "Jesus, Hailey, what did you do to your hair?"

"I highlighted it."

Chase took a swig. "I like it."

"It looks like a zebra committed suicide on your head," Meridian said. She paused for a moment and turned to me, a crooked smile on her lips. "I'm joking, Hailey. It looks good."

She turned back to Chase, twirling her hair between her fingers as she spoke, fiddling with the tail of Chase's shirt with the other hand. "So your parents are gonna be outta town this weekend, huh?"

"Yep." Chase smiled at her. "Maybe we should christen that jacuzzi of theirs."

I watched Meridan smile at Chase, wondering what in God's name he saw in her. Of course, she was pretty, but it was a fake, plastic sort of pretty. *Is that all it takes*, I thought, *to get a guy, a botched boob job and lips pumped fat with collagen?*

Meridian climbed off the hood of the Buick, glancing over at me as she straightened her denim skirt. "Guess we better head to class. Before that witch Thibodeaux climbs onto her broom."

*   *   *

After school, I asked Meridian to bring me to the hospital so I could see Iris's husband. She said I was crazy for visiting him, but I didn't care. I knew if I wanted to save my family, I was going to have to put a stop to Iris and my daddy's affair.

We got to the hospital around four or so. I knew Iris worked days at Nacho Mama's so I didn't have to worry about her throwing a wrench in my plan. Her husband's room was on the third floor. When I got to his door, I noticed his name, GARRETT GUIDRY, written on a piece of paper. I knocked, but no one answered. As I walked in, I could see him lying in the bed sleeping. He was skinny, so much that you could see the bones poking out from under his skin. His eyes were sunk deep in his skull, he had a crooked nose, and wires coming out of the veins on his hand. I'd heard Iris say he had cancer, so I expected him to be bald from the chemo, but he wasn't. He had a full head of black hair. It was so greasy, it looked like he'd combed it with an eel, and he had long sideburns and a patch of black hair peeking out the top of his hospital gown. He looked like Simon from *American Idol*, except for a black handlebar mustache and a mangled left hand that looked like someone shoved it through a meat grinder.

As I walked up to the bed, he peeked up at me through a cracked eye. "If you're the angel of death, for the love of God, take me now, please," he smiled, "before the damn hospital bill arrives."

The night before, I'd planned what I was going to say to him once I had him face to face. But for some reason, now that I was there, I couldn't bring myself to say it. I'm Hailey Trosclair, I wanted to say. I'm the girl whose daddy your wife's been humping while you've been wasting away in this bed. I opened my mouth, but all that came out was "I'm Hailey."

"I haven't seen you here before," he said.

"I'm a volunteer," I lied. "Here at the hospital."

"Shouldn't you be in a beauty pageant or something?" he said, "as pretty as you are?"

Without meaning to, I smiled back at him. *Why was he being so nice?* I thought. *Didn't he know he was dying of cancer?*

"You new?"

"Yeah," I lied again. "I just started."

"How do you like it so far?"

While he was talking I couldn't help but stare at the wires coming out of the black veins in his hand. "Huh?"

"Volunteering. How do you like it so far?"

"I like it just fine, I guess." As I got closer, I noticed his skin was oyster-grey. His lips were cracked and chapped, and his crooked nose was freckled with blackheads.

"It's nice. You taking time out to help people less fortunate than yourself."

"Well, I'm not that busy, really. All I do is go to school."

"Don't sell yourself short," he said, his grey hands folded over his belly. "Most kids your age are too selfish to make time for others. Most people for that matter. It's nice what you're doing. Helping people. You wanna sit down?"

"No. I can't stay long."

I walked over to a chair next to the bed, wanting to tell him what his terrible worm of a wife was doing, knowing, at the same time, that I could never tell such a nice person with cancer such a horrible thing.

"Just move my trousers to the side."

I grabbed his pants, put them on the end of the bed, and sat down in the chair.

"So, tell me about yourself, Hailey. I assume you live here in New Orleans?"

"Yeah," I answered, still staring at the wires coming out of the black veins in his hand. "I'm a sophomore at Ben Franklin."

As he spoke, sunlight crept through the window. "How do you like it so far?" he asked, his little swirl of black hair flickering in the light.

"It's alright, I guess."

"So, what are you, fourteen, fifteen?"

"I'm sixteen."

"Sixteen. That's a tough age. Everybody wanting you to act like an adult. Yet all they do is treat you like a child. Everybody talks about how wonderful it is to be a kid. Truth is, it's tough being young. You kids, you got it worse than us. All the drugs and everything. Kids toting guns to school. My generation had it easy. Compared to what you kids got to deal with."

I smiled.

"You'll have to excuse me. To be honest, I don't get many visitors. And when I do, I tend to talk their arms off."

"It's okay," I said, thinking how terrible it was that a man as nice as he was had to apologize for talking. Was Iris so busy off gallivanting with my father that she couldn't take one damn minute to come and talk to her own dying husband?

"Is there anything I can do for you?"

"Actually," he smiled, his rusty voice growing soft. "I'd do just about anything for a cigarette right now. I got a pack of GPCs down in the pocket of my trousers. Could you grab me one?"

I stood up and walked to the foot of the bed. "Is it okay? For you to smoke in here?"

"Not really," he said, gnawing his lip. "But I'll be quick. I just need a few drags is all."

I pulled the pack of GPCs from the pocket of his pants, shook a cigarette from the pack and handed it to him.

"There should be a lighter in the other pocket," he said, the GPC dangling from his lip.

I fished through the pocket of his pants until I found the lighter. "Here you go," I said, flicking the lighter near the tip of the cigarette.

He held the cigarette with the grey claw of his hand and took a long, deep drag. "Am I just a picture of health or what?" he asked, smiling through a silver puff of smoke. "A cancer patient smoking a cigarette. And in a hospital at that."

"Is that why you're here?" I asked him, as if I didn't know. "You have cancer?"

"Yep." He held the cigarette between his grey fingers and examined it, stared at it for a minute then took a long, deep drag. "Stomach cancer. At least that's what the doctors tell me."

"How did you find out? That you had cancer, I mean?"

"I got this pain in my gut. Didn't think much about it at first. Till it got worse." He flicked the ashes from his cigarette into a white styrofoam cup near his bed. "There ain't much they can do for me at this point." He smiled, exposing a mouthful of crooked teeth, "I'm a hopeless cause."

"There must be something they can do," I said. "Radiation. Chemo. Something."

He took another drag until the cigarette hissed. "You'd think so." He mashed the cigarette out on a pink packet of Sweet'N Low. "They already cut out part of my stomach, but somehow the cancer managed to make its way into my bloodstream. They said once it gets in your bloodstream, there really ain't much you can do."

As he spoke, I couldn't help but imagine the cancer, like a black seed sprouting in his gut.

"Do you have any children?"

"Nope." He wiped the sprinkle of ashes from his white hospital gown with a grey hand. "Me and my wife were planning to have a few kids at some point. But it doesn't look like that's gonna happen now. I'm really worried about her. My wife, I mean. I arranged my daddy's funeral, so I know what she's going through. Having to pick out a coffin. And a headstone. Then of course, you got to pay for it all. You wouldn't believe how much a coffin costs these days. Almost $5,000. Can you believe that? For a box that's not gonna do anything but rot in the ground. By the time you're done paying the hospital bills and the funeral costs, you can barely afford to die." Mr. Guidry smiled. "I told my wife she could toss me in a fire and throw my ashes to the birds if she wanted. Figured it would save us some money, you know. After all, what do I care about how the coffin looks? It's not like I'm gonna be alive to see it. I can't get over how expensive everything is these days. Back when I was young, dying was cheap. I remember when my grandfather died. They had the wake right there in the house."

"Really?"

"Yep. My daddy even built the coffin."

"It wasn't weird? Having a dead body in your house?"

Mr. Guidry reached a grey hand into a mason jar on the nightstand and pulled out a peppermint. "I guess it was a little weird. But you got to understand, we lived in the country. We didn't have enough money back then for all these fancy coffins and marble headstones." He put the mint in his mouth and dropped the crinkled wrapper on the nightstand, sucking on it as he spoke. "I remember going over to my grandaddy's house when I was a kid. He lived out near Amite. They were so poor they didn't even have running water."

"How did you use the bathroom?"

"You had to use the outhouse in the backyard."

"Did they have a telephone?"

"Nope." Mr. Guidry sucked on the peppermint between words. "No electricity either."

"What did they use for lights? Candles?"

"Yep. That and gas lanterns."

"That must have been terrible. No lights. No television. No

bathroom."

"Actually, it was kinda nice. At night, we'd all sit on the porch and tell stories. My grandaddy told the best stories."

"My daddy used to read me stories. When I was younger."

"Oh yeah?"

"Yeah. He read me *Moby Dick, Huckleberry Finn*. Even Shakespeare sometimes."

"He must be an English teacher or something, huh?"

"No. He just loves literature, that's all. He says it's important for a person to know all the classics."

"Does he read a lot? Your daddy?"

"He used to. Before my momma had her miscarriage. Now all he does is go down to the pool hall. Or the dog races. I think he and my mother may be getting a divorce."

"I'm so sorry to hear that, Hailey. I know how you feel. My parents got divorced when I was real young."

"Really?"

"Yeah. I was just about your age when my father left. He and my mother used to fight all the time. Came home one day from school and they were throwing knives at one another."

"Knives?"

"Yep. My father had to go to the emergency room that night. Got twenty-four stitches in his side. Another time, when he came home drunk, my mother hit him over the head with a frying pan. He said when she hit him, it felt like a thunderbolt going off in his head."

As Mr. Guidry was talking, a nurse with a crown of yellow hair poked her head in. "Time to check your pressure, Mr. Guidry." I motioned to Mr. Guidry that I had to leave.

"It was nice meeting you, Hailey," he said.

From the doorway, I glanced over my shoulder and watched as the nurse wrapped the blood pressure cuff around Mr. Guidry's bruised, grey arm.

"How ya feeling today, Mr. Guidry?" the nurse asked, patting her crown of yellow hair with a pale hand.

"Fine," he told her, smiling up at her with the same crooked-toothed smile. "I'm feeling just fine."

Chapter Seven

A pewter vase of red carnations was on the kitchen table, next to a torn piece of brown cardboard scrawled with the words: TO MAMA, LOVE CYRUS. I spent most of the evening in my room reading. Thumbing through the pages of *Our Town*, I found my hospital bracelet, from when I had pneumonia, stuck like a bookmark between the torn pages. I remembered how Mama and Daddy slept on cots at the hospital that night while the doctors took x-rays of my lungs. Sometimes I imagined I was sick again, with some terrible disease like leukemia. I'd imagine the pink ulcers blooming in my mouth, my eyes bulging in their bony sockets, the nausea moving over me in waves, all my hair burned off from the chemo, a few wiry black hairs sprouting like weeds from my bald, white skull.

Later that night, I woke to the sound of Mama yelling at Cyrus. When I got into the kitchen, she was holding the pewter vase in her hand.

"Would you tell me please, Cyrus," Mama asked, "what in God's name is this?"

A rose of blood blossomed in Cyrus's cheeks. "What are you squawking about now?"

"This vase you gave me. These flowers. They say IN LOVING MEMORY OF YELIAH DENNIS." Mama had taken the flowers out of the vase. She turned the vase upside-down and pointed to the words engraved in the pewter bottom. "Right here," she said, following each word with her finger as she read it. "In Loving Memory of Yeliah Dennis."

Cyrus stared at the pewter words. He didn't look up.

"Stealing flowers from a grave? I don't know where you get these ideas of yours. Certainly not from my side of the family, I can tell you that." She handed the vase to Cyrus.

"So, what? You don't want 'em?"

"No I don't want 'em. These flowers are for a dead woman, Cyrus. Do I look dead to you?"

Cyrus grabbed the vase from Mama and stormed out the house. Mama went into her bedroom and came back with the bouquet of red carnations in her hand. As she moved through the kitchen, red petals sprinkled the floor behind her. She opened the screen door and threw the flowers onto the lawn, slammed the door, and went back to her room. I decided to leave the trail of red petals on the kitchen floor hoping that Daddy would think Mama was being romantic.

When I went into Mama's room an hour or so later, she was sitting on the bed with a box of photographs spread out in front of her. "You okay, Mama?" I asked.

"Yeah, just looking at some pictures, that's all."

I walked over to Mama's bed and sat down next to her as she looked through the photographs. They were mostly pictures of me and Cyrus and a few from Mama and Daddy's wedding.

"You remember this one?" she asked, grabbing one of the photographs and passing it to me.

It was a picture of me and Cyrus at Disney World. Cyrus must have been about twelve or so. He'd lost over forty pounds after he started high school, but this was a picture of him before he'd lost the weight. His cheeks were pink and round, his arms like two fat pink sausages. He had a double-chin and a black wall of bangs that covered his pale forehead. A roll of fat hung over his belt. I was standing next to him, in a red flower dress, my hair in pigtails, a yellow and blue Daffy Duck visor pulled down over my eyes.

Mama grabbed another photograph from the pile of pictures and held it up, smiling. "Look how handsome your daddy was." The picture showed Daddy leaning against a green Mustang, his eyes shiny as pennies, the words JUST MARRIED spelled out in white shoe polish across the cracked rear windshield, a string of Schlitz cans dangling from the muffler. He was wearing a powder blue tuxedo and shiny black patent leather shoes.

Mama grabbed another photograph of Daddy smiling with a bottle of champagne overflowing in his hand.

"Did I ever tell you how your daddy asked me to marry him?"

I'd heard the story a thousand times, but for some reason, I never got sick of hearing it.

"Instead of just asking me to marry him, he got the Chinese man over at the China Garden to put a special message in my fortune cookie. I was so surprised when I cracked open that cookie and read those little black typed words: WILL YOU MARRY ME, MY LITTLE LAMB CHOP? That's what he used to call me, his Little Lamb Chop. He might have been broke and far from sophisticated, but he was so romantic. Really. He was. And thoughtful too."

"Can I ask you a question?"

Mama was still picking through the photographs. "Sure. What is it?"

"Do you think you and Daddy will ever get divorced?"

"Of course not. Why would you ask something like that?"

"I dunno. It just seems like you and Daddy have a lot of problems."

Mama pushed a strand of hair from my eyes and tucked it behind my ear. "Everybody's got problems, Hailey."

I couldn't help but feel bad for Mama, knowing that Daddy was sneaking around with that stupid redhead waitress behind her back.

"Meridian says that everybody who gets married eventually gets divorced."

"Yeah, well," Mama mumbled under her breath, "when you're married to a walking cathouse like Meridian's momma, you're probably better off getting divorced. Anyway, I didn't let my mother disown me so that I could turn around and divorce your father. And since when are you taking advice from Meridian? She's the last person you should be taking advice from."

"I never asked her for advice. She just said it one day. That marriages never work. No matter how hard people try. She said two people just aren't meant to spend their whole life together."

Mama licked her fingers as she thumbed through the photographs. "You shouldn't be hanging around with that girl, Hailey. She's just as loose and sneaky as her momma ever was."

"Yeah, but just because her momma was a slut doesn't mean Meridian's a slut."

"There's generations of sluttyness in Meridian's family. It got handed down to Meridian, the way some normal family might hand down a bum liver or a crooked nose. Her grandmother wasn't any different. Hatching litters of children with men they barely know. Smoking dope and God knows what else."

I couldn't believe that Mama had become so religious that she actually thought she was better than other people just because she went to church, and I thought it was funny that she mentioned smoking dope. I couldn't help but smile thinking of the time me and Meridian had smoked pot at Jazzland with those two head-bangers from St. Bernhard.

"The best thing you can do at this point is to stop hanging around her. Before her bad DNA rubs off on you." Mama grabbed a picture from the stack and passed it to me. "This one's from our honeymoon. When we went to Gulf Shores. I don't think you've seen that one before." The photograph showed Daddy standing on the beach in an orange plaid bathing suit, a white t-shirt draped over his shoulder. Mama said, as a joke, Daddy had spelled her name in suntan lotion on his chest. His skin was the color of red velvet cake, except for two white circles around his eyes where his sunglasses had been and the word LENA spelled out in white across his chest.

After Mama went to bed, I got on the Internet and looked up world religions. I read about Hinduism and Buddhism. I even read about this tribe in India that believed the dead souls of people lived inside certain fish. It said that women in the tribe who wanted to become pregnant ate the fish during a fertility ritual, believing the whole time that the dead soul of the person would be reincarnated from a fish into a newborn child. As I read this, I couldn't help but feel bad for Mama.

The next morning, I woke up, hoping to find Daddy asleep on the sofa, but he wasn't. I looked outside for his Nova, but all I saw was a patch of pale weeds where the car had been. The bouquet of dead carnations Mama had thrown on the lawn was still there. For the most part, the sky was empty, except for a grackle fluttering in the air, swooping down occasionally to peck at the dead petals.

Chapter Eight

That afternoon, the sky was the color of raw meat. Cyrus had asked if I'd take a ride with him down to the old bank to drop the statues off, and I was bored, so I decided to go. "Do me a favor," he said, his finger tracing a small lump on his neck. "Feel this." He reached over and grabbed my hand and placed my index finger on the lump in his neck. "Does that feel like something to you?"

"Jesus, Cyrus. It's just a lump, that's all."

"I know. That's what worries me. What if it's cancer or something?"

"It's not cancer," I said, staring out the car window, "Anyway, if it worries you so much, why don't you go see a doctor?"

"I hate doctors, you know that. What if they find something."

"Isn't that the point?"

Cyrus bit his lip as his finger traced the lump in his neck. "So what happened to Meridian?" he asked. "I thought she was coming along?"

"Nope." I reached over and opened the glove compartment and pulled Cyrus's Magic Eight Ball out. "You don't want to date a girl like Meridian, Cyrus."

Cyrus smiled. "Who says I wanna date her?"

"Anyway, I think she's dating Chase Haydel."

"Chase Haydel? The one whose parents own Haydel's Bakery? What's she dating him for?"

"I don't know. I think she likes his car. I try not to pay too much attention to what she does." I shook the eight ball. DOES CHASE THINK I'M CUTER THAN MERIDIAN? Slowly, the blue words came into focus. IT IS DECIDEDLY SO.

"Damn." Cyrus pulled a stick of ginseng gum from his pocket and bit off a piece. "I can't believe Meridian Fairfield's dating a Mexican."

"Chase's not a Mexican. He's white. He's just tan that's all. You think everybody who's got a tan is from Mexico?"

"He looks Mexican to me."

"He's just trying to look exotic, that's all."

"Is that all it takes to look exotic these days?" Cyrus asked. "A bottle of tanning cream?"

"I guess." I shook the magic eight ball again. IS CHASE EXOTIC? Again, the blue words came into focus. MOST LIKELY.

"I don't understand, if he's not Mexican, why the Hell is he trying to look Mexican."

"I dunno, maybe for the same reason you and all your friends dress like rappers."

"What's that supposed to mean?"

"I'm just saying, you and Lenny, and all of them, the way you dress, always quoting Ice Cube or some other rapper."

"Just 'cause I dress like a rapper doesn't mean I don't wanna be white."

"Well, maybe Chase doesn't like being white."

"What the Hell's wrong with being white?"

"Meridian hates being white. She says she wants to start getting those melatonin injections so her skin will be naturally brown. She says the worst thing you can be these days is white."

"That's just great," Cyrus said, staring in the mirror as he pressed his finger against the lump in his neck. "Just what I need. Another damn strike against me."

*   *   *

Later that night, we met Moses and his girlfriend Lilah down at IHOP. Lilah was a white girl with long stringy hair that looked more like rusted coils of wire sprouting from her skull than hair. She had silver caps on her front teeth, long pink fingernails that curled at the tips, and she was wearing tight jeans and a black bikini top so that you could see the C-section scar on her belly.

"How long's it take to get a damn cup of coffee around here?" she asked.

"Don't get your bowels in a bind, Woman," Moses told her. "She said she'd be right back." He tore a pack of sugar with his teeth and poured it into a cup of steaming coffee, stirring the coffee with a spoon as he smiled over at Cyrus, his face twisting into a smile. "Girl's got the patience of a piranha."

Moses stuffed a forkful of grits into his mouth, wiped his moustache with the sleeve of his shirt. "Any luck on those statues you were telling me about?"

"Yep," Cyrus told Moses. "Me and Hailey dropped 'em off at the bank earlier today."

"Good." Moses bit off a piece of bacon, stirring his grits with the other piece as he glanced up at Cyrus. "You hear anything about this baby molester in Algiers?"

"Nope." Cyrus picked up a menu and started looking through it.

"It was in the *Picayune* yesterday," Moses said, wiping his mouth with a napkin. "Bastard raped some little girl, got off due to lack of evidence." He took a drag off his cigarette then scooped some grits onto a piece of bacon and stuffed it into his mouth. As he bit off another piece, Lilah's hand grabbed a pack of sugar lying next to Moses's plate. In one quick move, Moses grabbed Lilah by the wrist, staring at her through the black worm holes of his eyes. "That's a good way to lose a hand, Woman."

Lilah looked up at Moses, dropped the sugar, and Moses let go of her hand. "Jesus Christ," Lilah snarled, "you liked to break my hand clean off."

"You looking for sympathy?" Moses asked her. "Try the dictionary. It's right between shit and syphilis." Moses snuffed his cigarette out in a yellow pile of scrambled eggs. "Don't turn ya eyes on me like that," he said, staring back at Lilah, his voice changing, as if someone had flipped a silver switch in his brain. "Less you wanna wind up in the meat wagon fore the night's over."

The table grew quiet. Moses took a sip of coffee, held up his hand, snapped his finger in the air, and the waitress hustled over to our table.

While Cyrus paid the check, I sat in the car, wondering if what we'd done would make the newspaper the next day. I imagined the words LOCAL BOY ACOSTED IN APARTMENT COMPLEX, a thick black headline across the front page, kids at school gossiping about what we'd done. As I sat there thinking, I looked over and noticed some of Cyrus's stuff in the cup holder between the seats. It was just some loose change, a crumpled receipt for an oil change, and his brass knuckles. I picked up the brass knuckles and slid them onto my hand. The metal was cool against my skin. I balled up my fist and stared at them, watching how glorious they looked flickering on my hand.

On the way home, Cyrus put "Ghetto Bird" by Ice Cube on repeat. I watched him tap the steering wheel as he sang to the music. All the while, I shook the eight ball, over and over, waiting for the blue words to appear.

WILL CHASE AND I HAVE SEX? . . . YES. DEFINITELY. DOES GOD REALLY EXIST? . . . DON'T COUNT ON IT. WILL MAMA AND DADDY GET DIVORCED? . . . SIGNS POINT TO YES.

*   *   *

After we got home, Cyrus went to bed, and I decided to watch TV for a while. *Taxi Driver* was on, and Robert De Niro was burning a bouquet of flowers in a sink. The roaches started crawling in my head again, and I started to feel like my thoughts were growing little feet and tip-toeing out of my head. I could feel little pinpricks of light behind my eyes, my muscles started to squirm like a black nest of moccasins, and my blood felt like chiggers wriggling under my skin. On TV, De Niro had shaved his head into a mohawk, and he was pointing a gun at Harvey Keitel. I smiled and mumbled "Suck on this," under my breath just before De Niro squeezed the trigger, and for a minute it almost sounded like De Niro's words were coming out of my mouth. I laid down on the sofa, and after a few minutes I started to feel like my thoughts were creeping back into my head. As I fell asleep, De Niro was smiling through the TV, pointing a bloody finger against his temple, as if it were the barrel of a loaded gun.

Chapter Nine

As Verma and I sat in the courtyard of her apartment complex, crows opened like black flowers in the trees. I watched her pick through the pieces of walnut shell in her palm, occasionally glancing up at a cluster of black clouds drifting across the horizon like little holes in the sky. I knew she was terrified of storms. Like most people in New Orleans, Verma had lived through Hurricane Camille, and whenever the sky turned black, or a hurricane started brewing in the Gulf, you could see the fear drifting across her face.

"There ain't no meat in these nuts," she said, tossing the pieces of walnut shell onto a patch of dead grass surrounding the green pool and then reaching down into the Chick-fil-A bag at her feet.

"You worried about the weather?"

"Little bit." She cracked the walnut with her teeth, put the pieces of shell in her lap. The pieces of walnut looked like little white bones. "I get nervous soon as the wind starts crawling through the trees. And the lightning sure as Hell don't help none."

"It scares me sometimes too," I told her. "When the wind picks up real fast."

"I know people say you're supposed to get butterflies in your stomach when you get nervous, but what I get feels more like a belly full of tumors eating at my insides. The nerves start jumping in my head and before long I get so scared I can't stand it." Verma grabbed a handful of walnuts from the bag and spilled them into her robe pocket. "Anyway, enough about the weather. Tell me what you been up to? You do anything interesting last night?"

"Just hung out with Cyrus. Down at the old bank."

"Why you wanna go down there?" She put the cracked walnut in her lap, her shriveled brown fingers picking through the pieces of walnut. "You don't need to get tangled up with them slick-assed boys, Hailey. You better than that."

"I was just hanging out with them, that's all."

Verma put the last few pieces of walnut in her mouth and brushed off her apron. "I seen them saggy-ass boys your brother hangs out with. They got the souls of a shook chicken egg. And that Moses character he's been running with. Hell, that creepy bastard could spook the chords out a guitar." She was rubbing her legs with her hands as she spoke. "I've told you time and time again, Hailey, about getting tangled up with hoodlums like that."

I pulled a handful of walnuts from the bag at Verma's feet and spilled them onto the ground. "Your legs hurting again?" I asked. I grabbed a walnut and cracked it with my teeth, picking through the broken shell in my palm.

Verma rolled her stockings down and scratched her legs with her fingernails. The stockings looked like tourniquets wrapped around her ankles. "Yeah." She sighed. "They sleep again." She wiped her robe clean and pulled a Chesterfield from the pocket. "Blood don't move through my legs like it used to." She yawned behind her ashy brown hand, then took a drag of her Chesterfield, a white string of smoke slithering out of her mouth as she spoke. "Got an appointment on Friday with the doctor." Her face tightened into a brown fist. "Place gives me the creeps. All them doctors with their damn stethoscopes creeping all over your bones. They laid hands on me last Sunday down at the church. Prayed to God, and asked Him to save my leg." She took another drag, speaking around the cigarette. "But I barely got any feeling left in it these days."

"Hopefully, the doctor'll help you get the feeling back. I'm sure he'll have some kind of medicine that'll help."

"Yeah. I'm hoping." Verma rolled up her stockings, the Chesterfield stuck in the side of her mouth. "By the way, tell your daddy that friend of mine over at Wal-Mart called. He told me your daddy didn't show up for that interview. As soon as I get back from the doctor, me and your daddy gonna take ourselves a trip down to Wal-Mart. You be sure to tell him I haven't forgot."

I smiled. "I'll tell him." I cracked another walnut with my teeth, spilled the white bones of the walnut in the palm of my hand. "Can I ask you something, Verma?"

"Sure." Verma tapped her cigarette, and a long grey ash sprinkled the ground. "What's on your mind?"

"Do you think my momma and daddy will ever get divorced?"

"Naw. Your momma and daddy been married for a long time."

I ate the last piece of walnut, threw the empty shell into a patch of ferns. "I think Daddy's cheating on Mama."

"What makes you think that?" Verma asked.

"Well, the other night, he was all drunk, and he asked me to drive him to the Circle K over on Marigny."

"Uh huh." Verma took a drag off the Chesterfield, her eyes squinted.

"Thing is, once we got there, he didn't go to the Circle K. He went to that strip club next door instead."

"Not the She She Lounge?"

"Yeah, that's it. Anyway, eventually this red-headed woman came out, and they started talking. She's a waitress over at Nacho Mama's. I could hear them talking, and I think she was asking Daddy to leave Mama."

"I'm sure you musta heard wrong, Hailey. I've been knowing your daddy a long time. Trust me, he ain't going nowhere. That's just your daddy's way. He's been trying to get back at your momma for years."

"Get back at her? Get back at her for what?"

Verma paused. "That's just your daddy's way. Stop worrying so much. You too young to worry so much, Hailey."

"Get back at Mama for what?"

Verma rubbed her bloodshot eyes with her hands, mumbling under her breath.

"Get back at her for what, Verma?"

"Dammit, that's your momma's business, Hailey. It ain't my place."

"Tell me."

Verma tilted her head, rubbing her forehead with her hand. "I'm so sorry, Hailey. I thought you already knew."

"Knew what?"

"Your momma said she told you."

"Told me what? Verma, please."

"Your momma. She cheated on your daddy when they first got married. All right. There it is."

"Mama cheated on Daddy?"

"Yes, but she was young and stupid. Your momma was sixteen when they got married. She was just a child."

"I can't believe this. I can't believe I didn't know my own mother cheated on my father."

"Don't go getting mad at your momma now, Hailey. Not till you walked in her shoes."

"All this time I blamed Daddy."

"There ain't no one to blame, Hailey. They your parents. People make mistakes. You can't go around blaming people for how your life turns out. The only person you got to blame for how your life turns out is you."

As Verma spoke, I thought about how mad I was at Mama, about how Daddy had kept Mama's dirty little secret all those years.

"Listen to me, Hailey. Your momma and daddy been together for a long time, and they love each other. Very much."

"I don't understand. If they love each other so much, why are they cheating on each other? People who love one another don't cheat on each other."

"Just 'cause they make a mistake don't mean they don't love each other. People do stupid things sometimes, Hailey. Things they regret. Haven't you ever done anything you regret?"

"Yeah."

"Well, alright then." Verma snuffed out her cigarette, and I helped her out of the rocking chair. "Come inside and peel some potatoes with me. It'll help get your mind off all this business."

I was so pissed at Verma for keeping that secret from me, and I sure as Hell wasn't in any mood to peel potatoes. She told me she was sorry again, and I kissed her on the cheek and headed home.

*   *   *

When I got to the house, the rain had stopped, and the sky was the same terrible blue as Jesus' eyes. Daddy and Cyrus were arguing about a T-bone that was missing from the refrigerator, and I was bored, so I decided to put my bathing suit on and lay out in the yard.

A small halo of sunlight had finally blinked through the clouds when I heard a car pull up. As I sat up in the lounge chair, I saw Chase's black Firebird flickering in the sun. I stared at him from behind the black lenses of my Ray-Bans as he drifted across the yard. When he walked up, I was rubbing tanning lotion on my stomach.

"They got tanning beds for that, you know," Chase said, pulling a lighter the shape of a small hand grenade from his shirt pocket, an unlit cigarette dangling from his lip. "Not to mention pills."

"I'm not going to any leper colony. If that's what you're here for."

He cupped his hands, pressed the trigger of the hand grenade lighter and lit the cigarette. "Meridian asked me stop by and pick you up. She wants to go over to the arcade. You up for it?"

"Sure. Lemme grab my flip-flops and my purse."

When I came back, Chase was waiting for me in his Firebird. He said he had to stop off at his place on the way.

He lived with his parents in a fancy house off Magazine Street. The house looked like something off MTV Cribs. The dining room had a huge alabaster chandelier with a gold and bronze fleur-de-lis hanging above a statue of a naked woman with a piece of her nipple chipped off. The bathrooms were all marble, with jacuzzis, gold sinks and gold toilets. In the backyard, there was even a swimming pool the shape of a blue kidney.

Chase's room was upstairs. There was a coffee table in the center of the room. On the coffee table, a cigarette butt with lipstick on the end had been snuffed out on a blue poker chip, and two contact lenses were floating in a pair of shot glasses.

Chase reached into a small refrigerator and grabbed a Zima. "Wanna drink?"

"Sure." I pulled a compact and a tube of lipstick from my purse and Chase walked over and handed me the bottle then sat down on the sofa.

"So, I never did ask you?" he said, smiling at me with his little red doll's mouth. "How'd you and Meridian meet?"

"I met her in Ms. Thibodeaux's class." I could feel his eyes creeping all over me. As I took a sip of beer, I heard a cell phone with a My Chemical Romance ring tone. When I looked down, I noticed a red, white, and blue British flag cell phone vibrating across the coffee table.

Chase walked over to the table and grabbed it, hissing through his teeth as he reached down for it. "Damn back's killing me." He stood there for a moment, looking at the cell phone.

"How'd you hurt it?"

"Scoliosis. I've had it since I was a kid."

"Me too."

"Really?" He picked up the cell phone, flashed a crooked smile then hung it up. "Bet yours is not as bad as mine." He turned around and lifted his silk shirt. He had a purple-yellow bruise in the middle of his back. When he lifted his arm, a thin pink scar puckered between his ribs. "Pretty bad, huh?"

"Yep." My eyes followed the ripple of muscles flexing beneath his candied yam skin.

"I got a thirty degree curve in my spine," he said, turning around and lowering his shirt. "Yours can't be that bad."

I turned around, so that Chase was standing behind me.

"Jesus," he said, his voice warm on my neck. "Your spine's as crooked as a politician."

I felt him get closer. He didn't say anything for a moment. Then, I felt the tip of his finger touch the small of my back, tracing the curve of my spine. I glanced over my shoulder and saw him in the corner of my eye. He wasn't looking at my spine. He was looking up, the way a doctor looks up while his fingers search for a lump of cancer.

"I gotta admit," he said, his voice like a hummingbird fluttering against my neck. "I got a thing for stuff like this."

"A thing for what? Crooked spines?"

"Yeah. Crooked spines, C-section scars. Any kind of imperfection."

I smiled. "You're so twisted."

I could feel his right hand flirting with the yellow bow of my bikini top while his other hand slid around my waist toward my stomach. When I felt his hand moving toward my bikini top, I pulled away quickly and slapped him on the mouth.

"Jesus," he snarled, licking his lips. "Why the Hell'd you do that?"

I looked up and noticed a thin line of blood on his lip. His two front teeth were stained red. I raised my hand and touched his lip with the tip of my finger and he flinched. "I'm sorry," I said. "Wait. You can kiss me. Really. I want you to."

"What? So you can belt me again?"

"No. Really. I'm sorry. You can kiss me. Really. I want you to."

He looked at me for a moment, then leaned in and kissed me. His mouth was hard, his lips cracked and chapped, and his breath tasted like a warm stew of Zima and French fries. I kissed him for a moment and pulled away gently, looking up at him. "You ever think about God?"

"Nah. My father was a biologist. We worshipped Darwin in my house."

"You know Darwin became a Christian before he died?"

"No he didn't."

"Yes he did. He converted to Christianity on his deathbed. I've actually been thinking about getting saved myself."

Chase grabbed the cigarette from the bar, took a drag and smiled. "Saved from what?"

I laughed. "Saved. You know, baptized. My mother says you got to get saved if you want to go to Heaven. Figure I might as well do it now while I'm young, case I drop dead or something."

"To tell the truth, I'm not that religious. I kinda like astrology, though."

"Jesus, don't mention astrology around my mother. She thinks it's the devil's work."

"Really?"

"Yep. She's kind of obsessed with religion."

"Has she always been like that?"

"No. She lost a baby a few months back, and she's been obsessed with religion ever since. She used to be kind of fun actually, before she found religion."

As I said this, I could feel hase's cell phone vibrating against my hip. A second later, I could feel his hand groping for it. "That's Meridian," he said, clipping the cell phone to his belt. "We better skedaddle."

* * *

When we pulled up to Meridian's house, she came out wearing a jean skirt, a skimpy stars and stripes halter top, and silver hoop earrings. "What's up, Bitches?" she winked, pulling a clove cigarette from her purse and lighting the tip. She opened the passenger side door, and I climbed into the backseat of the Firebird.

"So." Meridian turned to Chase. "Did you miss me?" She took a drag off her cigarette, resting her hand on Chase's shoulder.

Chase smiled. "I missed parts of you."

Meridian slapped Chase's shoulder jokingly, planted a kiss on his cheek, then turned around. "Did you see the bracelet Chase bought me, Hailey?" She held up her hand so I could see the diamond bracelet flickering around her wrist. "Ain't it just about the prettiest goddamn bracelet you've ever seen?" She leaned over and whispered something in Chase's ear, but I couldn't hear what she said. "Oh, by the way." She reached into her purse. "I got some change for us. For the arcade. Hold onto it for me. You know me. I'll lose it."

Meridian reached over the seat, and I held out my palm as she spilled a fistful of coins into my hand. I'd forgotten I'd touched Chase's bloody lip. While we rode down Paris Road, I picked through the pile of change in my palm, glancing occasionally at the drop of dried blood—like a perfect red period at the end of my finger.

Chapter Ten

The next day, I asked Cyrus to drive me to the hospital so I could see Iris's husband again. I'd told him one of my teachers was in the hospital and that I wanted to go and see her. I wasn't sure why I wanted to see Mr. Guidry again. I guess I felt sorry for him, knowing that he was dying and all. The day before, I'd gotten a book from the school library about how certain diets can help people beat cancer. I figured Mr. Guidry might be interested in it so I brought it with me to the hospital in my knapsack. We got to the hospital around noon or so, and when I got to Mr. Guidry's room, I found him sitting up in his bed, reading a book.

"Hailey," he said, folding his grey hands in his lap. "It's so good to see you."

"How are you feeling, Mr. Guidry?"

He smiled, exposing a row of crooked teeth. "Better than most cancer patients, I assume."

I kissed him on his grey cheek and sat down in the chair next to his bed.

"You aren't sick of me yet?" he asked.

"Nope. I even brought you a present."

"A present," he said. "You didn't have to do that."

I handed the book to him and he opened it in his lap, licking his fingers as he thumbed through the pages.

"It's a book," I told him. "It talks about how you can change your diet. So you can beat your cancer."

Mr. Guidry paused for a moment and then closed the book. "Hailey, thank you for the book, but I think you may have misunderstood me."

"It talks about certain foods you can eat," I told him. "It says there's certain foods that can help people beat their cancer."

"Hailey, sit back for a moment. Please."

I did as Mr. Guidry asked.

"First of all, thank you very much for the book. It's very nice of you to think of me. But you have to understand, Hailey. I've been diagnosed with end-stage cancer. There's really nothing they can do for me at this point."

"I know. But the book talks about people who beat their cancer, even after the doctors told them they were going to die."

"It's okay, Hailey. I'm okay with dying. I know it's hard for you to understand. But I've had a lot of time to think about this. It wasn't sudden. Like I told you, I've been knowing for months that I had this cancer. Over time, I've come to accept it. I know it's hard for you to understand."

"Yeah, but don't you even wanna try to beat it?"

"I can't beat it, Hailey. If the doctors would have caught it earlier, I might have had a chance. They just caught it too late is all. But I'm okay with it."

"If you don't think changing what you eat will help, maybe you could try praying? Maybe if you prayed to Jesus, he'd cure your cancer? My momma says the preacher down at our church has cured plenty of people."

"To tell the truth, I'm not very religious. I like to tell people I'm a recovering Catholic."

Mr. Guidry told me about St. Agnes, the Catholic school he'd gone to when he was a boy, how the nuns made him kneel in rice when he talked in class, how when he went to confession every month he could actually smell the booze on the priest's breath. He even showed me the scar on his belly where the doctor had cut out a piece of his stomach.

*   *   *

Cyrus and I were nearly halfway home when I noticed a police car in the rearview mirror. As we turned onto Elysian Fields, the squad car flipped on its lights, and a skinny white arm reached out the window and motioned for us to pull over. Cyrus pulled over to the side of the road, near a patch of dead weeds and climbed out the car. The policeman, some yellow-haired, skinny man with pocked skin, walked up and asked Cyrus his name. Cyrus waved his driver's license in the policeman's face, and after he checked Cyrus's insurance, he told Cyrus he wanted to speak to him down at the precinct. Cyrus did like the deputy said and followed him down to the station.

When we got there, the officer brought Cyrus and me into a white room with glass walls. A few minutes later, another man came in and sat down. He was an older fat man with a stubbly chin and a bald, liver-spotted skull. He had tiny baby teeth that looked like someone had plugged little white Chiclets into his gums, and you could smell Old Spice seeping from his pores. His hips looked wider than they were supposed to be, like he'd had someone else's hips welded onto his skeleton, and his chest looked like Brandon Piggert's chest the summer he'd grown little midget boobs after shooting up a batch of steroids. The skin on his face was pocked, and it reminded me of the girl's face from *The Exorcist*. I smiled thinking of the police officer vomiting up chunks of green pea soup, his head spinning around on his neck, a priest dousing him with bottles of Old Spice.

"Did Calvin tell you why we brought you down for questioning?" he asked, massaging his little midget boob with the inside of his wrist.

"I just told him we had some questions for 'em," the yellow-haired cop said. "Didn't tell 'em what it was regarding."

"Well." The policeman made a steeple of his hands. "We got word last week that some statues were stolen from a cemetery in New Orleans." He pulled a cigarette from his shirt pocket and grabbed a match from behind his ear. "We got reason to believe it was some boys from the Gentilly area." He struck the match with his fingernail and lit the tip, tossed the match in a glass ashtray on the table. "You wouldn't know anything about that, now would you?"

"No sir," Cyrus felt his shirt pocket for a cigarette, pulled out an empty pack and crushed it in his fist. "Can I bother you for a cigarette?"

The cop pulled a cigarette from his shirt pocket and handed one to Cyrus. "What kind of statues were they?" Cyrus asked.

"Mostly religious ones." The police officer took a drag of his cigarette, squinting at Cyrus as he spoke. "Believe there's one of a angel. And another one of a nun. That right, Calvin?"

"Yep. And one of a boy holding a rosary I think." The yellow-haired officer licked his finger, thumbing through a stack of papers as he spoke. "Three statues total."

The fat officer flicked the ashes from his cigarette into the glass ashtray on the table and glanced up at Cyrus. "Thing is. Someone spotted a car similar to yours at the scene." He took a drag of his cigarette and smiled with his little baby Chiclets teeth, turned to the cop* then tuned back to Cyrus. "You could see why we mighta thought you were involved."

"Yes sir," Cyrus said. "But I can assure you. I never stole any statues."

The cop stared at Cyrus for a moment, scratching an itch on his liver-spotted skull, the smell of Old Spice seeping from his skin like mustard gas. "You wouldn't happen to know who did it, would you?"

"No sir," Cyrus told him. "I heard someone was stealing statues from some graveyard in New Orleans. But it wasn't me. Dead people give me the creeps."

The police officer turned his eyes on me. "This your sister here?"

"Yes sir. Hailey's her name."

The police officer snuffed his cigarette out in the ashtray, rubbing his stubbly chin as he spoke. "I'm sure a sweet girl like you don't know anything about any stolen statues."

"No sir. I heard about it. Like Cyrus said. But I never heard who did it."

The fat cop turned to Cyrus. "You wouldn't mind if we came over to your house and looked around a bit, would you? Just to be sure?"

"No sir," Cyrus told him. "We're not hiding any statues."

"It's just standard procedure, you understand. Just to be sure."

*   *   *

On the way home, I told Cyrus I was scared that the police would find out what we'd done. He said I shouldn't worry, that the police were just fishing for leads. Luckily, when we got to the house, Daddy wasn't home. After the police officers climbed out of their squad car, they asked Cyrus to open the garage. Cyrus unhooked the latch, and opened the garage door, and the police officers walked in, the fat one taking off his sunglasses and sticking them in his shirt pocket as he stepped over a pile of boxes.

"Somebody needs to take a rag to this place," he mumbled under his breath, swatting at a silver spider web. As he stepped over an ice chest, he pulled a wooden match from behind his ear and stuck it in the side of his mouth. He walked over to a porcelain toilet that was wedged between an old stained mattress and a wooden desk, reaching down between the toilet and the mattress. "You know you got a Bible down here?"

"Oh yeah," Cyrus yelled from the doorway of the garage. "That's my momma's. It musta gotten misplaced, I guess."

The police officer pulled the Bible out. "Don't seem like any place for a holy book." He wiped the dust off the cover of the Bible and placed it on the table next to him. He walked a few more steps, then stepped over a stack of plywood until he got to Daddy's drill press, then ran a hand across the drill press, wiping away tiny bits of rust and dirt. "My daddy had a drill press like this," he said, wiping his spotted hand on his pants. "They don't make 'em like this anymore." In the corner of the garage, the yellow-haired officer was examining an old blue exercise bike of Mama's. The fat officer stepped over a laundry basket and a stack of cinder blocks, then strolled past a folded ping-pong table, fishing through a box of screws as if he was shopping for something at a yard sale. He grabbed a chess piece from the box and held it to his nose, like he was smelling it. "What's that back there?" he asked, pointing the white chess piece toward a pile of silver rims.

"They're rims, for my car." Cyrus smiled. "Owning rims is not against the law, is it?"

The police officer didn't answer Cyrus, only picked at his little baby Chiclets teeth with the dead match, then placed the chess piece back in the box.

"Looks clean," the yellow-haired cop said, staring at purple doubloon he'd found in an old box of Mardi Gras beads.

The cop twirled the wooden match in the corner of his mouth for a moment then started to walk back toward the door of the garage. When he got to the doorway, he placed a hand on Cyrus's shoulder. "We'll get back to you. If we got any more questions." The police officers walked across the rutted yard and headed back into their squad car, turned the car around, and headed down the clam-shell driveway.

*   *   *

That night, when we got down to the old bank, Moses wasn't there yet because he'd gone down to Broad Street to sell his plasma. Cyrus said Moses had been selling his blood for years, and that half of New Orleans probably had Moses's blood running through their veins. Eventually he showed up, and for some reason he was all pissed off about that kid who'd molested that girl in Algiers. They smoked a few joints, and Cyrus told Moses that he'd talked to a friend of his that knew the kid, and that the kid hung out at a bar in Algiers called The Old Point Bar. Moses said they should go over to Algiers, find that kid, and beat the Word of God into his nappy head. Cyrus laughed, and a few beers later, we were on our way to Algiers.

The Old Point Bar was on Patterson Street. Cyrus and Moses parked their cars in the lot outside the bar, and I stayed in the car while they went inside. I must have fallen asleep because the next thing I knew Cyrus was knocking on the car window yelling at me to open the door. As I leaned over to open the door, I noticed a kid standing next to Cyrus that I'd never seen before. He looked fragile, like his bones were made of glass. His skin was pink, like the inside of a seashell, and his eyes were cornflower blue.

When Cyrus opened the door, the kid climbed in and closed the door behind him. Cyrus walked around the car and climbed into the driver's seat. "Cory, Hailey. Hailey, Cory."

The kid was holding a martini in his left hand. Cyrus cranked the engine, put the Hyundai in drive, and Moses followed us out of the lot and onto Hwy 59.

"So," the kid asked, sucking on the olive's pimento from his martini, "where's this party at anyway?"

"It's not far," Cyrus told him. "Just sit back and relax. We'll be there before you know it."

The kid turned to me as he took a sip of his martini, smiling, the tiny black hairs of his peach fuzz mustache hanging over his upper lip. He glanced out the window and looked forward again.

"You said it was in Algiers, right?" the kid asked.

"Yep." Cyrus bit at a hangnail. As he changed the track on the CD player, the kid put the martini between his legs, turned the yellow collar of his shirt up, and slouched down in his seat. He was short, and when he slouched down in his seat, I could see the top of his head. His shiny black hair was parted down the middle, and the crooked line of white scalp looked like a crack in his skull.

Cyrus bit his lip as he tapped the steering wheel, clicking his teeth, as if a thought was ticking like a bomb in his head. He drove for a while until he came to an empty lot littered with old car parts and rotted tires. With Moses following us, we turned onto the gravel road that led to the back of the lot. When Cyrus reached a gutted yellow Chevy speckled with grey primer propped up on cinder blocks, he slowed down and killed the engine. As he opened his door, the kid sat up in his seat, and the overhead light came on. His martini had spilled all over his jeans. "Where are we?" he asked.

"Get out." Cyrus stepped out of the car and came around to the passenger's side, opened the door, and grabbed the kid by his shirt. "Just shut up and get out."

"Where? Where are we?" The kid asked, fear falling across his face.

Cyrus pulled the kid from the car, kicked the door shut, and led him to the front of the car, the way a farmer might lead a pig to slaughter. By now, Moses had gotten out of his car. I could see his shadow dragging by the window, gravel crackling beneath his feet as he walked by.

The next thing I knew, Moses was standing in the yellow glow of Cyrus's headlights punching the kid in the stomach while Cyrus held the kid by the collar. Without even thinking, I climbed out of the car, walked up to the kid and slapped him across the face. "You like raping little girls?" I asked him. "I'm a girl. Why don't you rape me, you goddamn pedophile?" A second later, Cyrus handed the kid off to Moses and stepped in closer, the brass knuckles flickering in the black air as Cyrus punched the kid in the ribs. Cyrus was hitting him so hard I thought the kid's bright blue eyes were going to roll out of his head. The kid was yelling now, his voice like a stuck pig. Cyrus hit him again, and the kid fell to the ground, lifting his head as he crawled across the rain-eaten dirt. He had a handful of dirt clenched in his fist, and his hair was tangled with leaves. All the while he was screaming, his voice haunting the black air as Moses and Cyrus took turns kicking him in the ribs.

Cyrus kicked him one last time, then stepped back for a moment, catching his breath. "Whatcha wanna do with him?"

"Leave him be," Moses said. He pulled a blue comb from his afro, yanked it through the black hairs of his moustache then stuck it back in his afro. "He can crawl his way back to the bar for all I care."

On the way home, Moses said he needed gas, so we stopped at the Circle K before heading back to New Orleans. I followed him into the store while Cyrus pumped gas, grabbed myself a Milky Way and a hot dog for Cyrus, and made my way to the register. When I got to the register, Moses was in line. He put a Red Bull on the counter, reached over a rack of Zapp's Potato Chips and unscrewed a jar of pig lips.

"Ain't nothing like a pig lip and Red Bull after a good ass-kicking," he mumbled, his hand fishing through the pink water for the perfect lip.

When we got back outside, Moses told Cyrus to meet him over at his place. On the way to New Orleans East, I thought about what we'd done. For the first time in my life, I was starting to feel a power that I'd never known before. For so long, I'd listened to Mama pray for God, hoping he'd cure our family, but Moses and Cyrus didn't pray for anything. They'd gone and found the person who was a sinner, and when they'd found them, they punished him the way a sinner deserved to be punished. I knew it wasn't right, but I have to admit, it was kind of exciting.

Chapter Eleven

The yard surrounding Moses's lime green trailer was littered with old car parts, rotten tires, rusty rims, and dented car fenders. The windows of the trailer were covered with aluminum foil, and the inside smelled like mildew. Moses had a plasma TV in the corner of the room. On the wall, above the TV, was a velvet painting of Jesus with white wings. In the painting, Jesus was holding his palms out, revealing the bloody nail holes in each of his hands. In the other corner was a black La-Z-Boy chair. The floor was covered with thick green shag carpet. A black cat with yellow eyes stretched over the arm of a red vinyl chair, pawing at the missing head of a Barbie doll. On the floor was what looked like a bong made out of yellow hamster tubing and duct tape.

When we walked in, the room was dark, and Moses was sitting on the purple velvet sofa, in the blue light of the television, a pack of Zig Zag rolling papers on the coffee table in front of him.

"I've been jonesing for some dope all night," Moses said. He held the joint up to his mouth, licked the length of the paper, then twisted the joint closed.

Cyrus sat down on the black La-Z-Boy chair in the corner and popped open a bottle of Purple Haze.

A small roach that looked like a tiny brown jewel scurried across the coffee table. Moses followed it with his eyes, waiting for it to stop, and then smashed it with his clenched fist. "It's some good dope," he said, wiping yellow roach guts on his pants. "Black Ganja. Straight from Jamaica." He pulled the lighter from his robe pocket, lit the joint, and took a long drag. "Got it from Cedric." He took one more long toke and passed the joint to Cyrus "That boy can get some good dope. Lemme tell you."

Cyrus held the joint in his hand for a moment, as if he was studying it, then took a long drag. "Damn that's some good shit," he wheezed, coughing into his hand and quickly giving it back to Moses. "Here you go, Miss Hailey," Moses said, smiling with his dirty teeth as he handed the joint to me, a tangled string of white smoke creeping out of his mouth. "Don't hog it now."

I looked at the joint, then glanced over at Cyrus.

"No way, Hailey," Cyrus said, swallowing a gulp of Purple Haze. He picked up the remote control and started flipping through the channels. "You're way too young to be smoking pot."

"Not so fast, Cyrus. Hailey can make up her own mind." Moses smiled, his gold tooth flickering in the blue light of the television. "Whatcha say, Miss Hailey? You old enough to do what you want. Ain't you?"

Cyrus shook his head, then turned his eyes back on the television, flipping through the channels. Cyrus didn't know it, but I'd smoked pot twice with Meridian, once at the State Fair, and once behind the gym during fourth period. I held the joint in my hand for a moment, then took a long drag. The minute I sucked the smoke into my lungs, I started to cough.

We all took a few more drags and Moses snuffed what was left of the joint out in a gold tin ashtray on the coffee table. A few minutes later, my head started to tingle, and I started to feel like my thoughts were leaking out of my skull. As I sat there, I imagined little white clouds of pot smoke, like tiny ghosts, floating around in my head, haunting my thoughts.

"I gotta go check on my momma." Moses said. "You wanna meet her?"

"Your mother?" I asked. "She's here?"

"Yeah. Her room's in the back. Come tell her hello. She loves meeting new people."

The trailer was a double-wide. I followed Moses until we came to a bedroom. When I got to the doorway, I could see an old black woman lying in the bed. She was bony with bifocals, and her hands were knotted with arthritis. Her skull was caved in a little on one side, and the wrinkled skin around her mouth made it look like her lips had been sewn shut.

"That you, Moses?" the woman asked, staring up at us through her bifocals.

"Yeah, Momma. It's me." Moses turned to me. "Her eyes are shot."

"You home for the night?" she asked.

"Yeah, Momma. I'm home for good."

"You got somebody with you there?"

"Yeah. This is Hailey."

The lady held out a wrinkled brown hand. Her cheeks were smeared with rouge, and she had lipstick on her teeth. I walked over, leaned down, and put my hand in hers.

"It's nice to meet you, Hailey. My name's Idouma. I'm Moses's momma." Her breath smelled like dirty diapers.

"You hungry, Momma?" Moses asked.

"Yeah. Maybe some soup. We got vegetable?"

"I think so. I'll go look." Moses motioned to me that he'd be right back.

I stared at the lady's eyes. They were the color of greasy dishwater. Moses had told me that his mother had a pacemaker. I imagined a tiny metal box in her chest humming like a hive of bees.

"How do you know Moses, Honey?" she asked.

"I met him though my brother, Cyrus. Moses says he's been taking care of you, huh?"

"Oh yeah," she said. "Moses takes wonderful care of me. He's my baby you know."

"Really?"

"Yep." Her greasy dishwater eyes flickered. "Had him when I was sixteen. Raised five kids all by myself." She smiled. She had lost all her teeth and her gums were purple. "You got any brothers and sisters? Other than the one knows Moses?"

"No. Just Cyrus and I."

"Just you two huh? I tell ya, people sure don't have as many kids as they used to. It's too expensive for one thing. I got nine brothers and sisters. You believe that? Nine. People in the neighborhood used to call my momma a baby factory."

"Do you still talk to them, your brothers and sisters?"

"Heaven's no. Only got one left. And she lives in Texas. Rest of 'em passed."

"I'm sorry."

"You ain't got no reason to be sorry. They all lived good lives. All of 'em." She smiled with her purple gums. "When you get old as we are, dying ain't so bad. Not after you lived a long life like we done lived."

"It was nice meeting you."

"You going? But you just got here."

"Yeah. My brother's probably ready to go."

"Well, it was nice meeting you, Sweetie."

When I got back to the den, Cyrus had fallen asleep. I grabbed the remote from his lap and started flipping through the channels. A minute or so later, I heard a microwave beep, and I saw Moses walking from the kitchen with a bowl of soup. He was gone for about fifteen minutes or so, and when he came back, he sat down and popped open a Purple Haze.

"I didn't know your mother lived with you," I said, flipping through the channels.

"Yep. Been taking care of her for the last few years or so."

"She seems nice."

"Yeah. Just old that's all. How old are you, Miss Hailey?" Moses asked, licking the beer from his fingers. "If you don't mind me asking."

"Sixteen."

He wiped his mouth with the tail of his shirt. I could see he had a tattoo on his chest, but I couldn't make out what it was. "I got a daughter turned fifteen just last month."

"Really? I didn't know you had a daughter."

"Yep. She stays over with her momma mostly. Over in Algiers."
He took a sip of Purple Haze, reached down and scratched the yellow-eyed cat next to his feet. "I don't get to see her as much as I'd like. You kinda remind me of her. Some of your mannerisms."

"When was the last time you saw her?"

"Been a few months, I guess."

"You must miss her."

"Yeah. I miss her a whole lot. We was thick as thieves, me and her."
He took another swig of beer. "When she was little I used to hold her in the crook of my arm, while I was driving. She didn't weigh no more than six pounds when she was born. She had these tiny little toes. Looked more like little black-eyed peas than toes really. And black, black hair. Doctor said he'd never seen a baby with so much hair."

"She goes to school over in Algiers?"

"Yeah. Bethune Elementary. Spose to go to McDonogh 35 next year. Less that chicken-hearted momma of hers decides to move away."

"Who? Your ex-wife?"

"Ex-girlfriend. She's been threatening me for years. Saying she's gonna move away and take my daughter from me."

"Can she do that? Move away with your daughter, I mean?"

"I spose so. A man don't have much rights when it comes to the law. Seems like most judges side with the mother. Specially when the man's got a record like mine."

"Where did she threaten to move?"

"Biloxi. She's got a uncle out there works at one of the casinos. Says he can get her a job as a blackjack dealer. Says she can live with him rent free, till she gets on her feet. It's probably for the best, since the job she's got now don't pay much."

"Where does she work now?"

"Over at the paper mill in Algiers. Don't get me wrong, the paper mill pays good. But she could make twice what she's making as a dealer in Biloxi."

"What's your daughter's name?"

"Africa."

"That's a pretty name."

"Yeah. Name suits her too."

I could see his blood-shot eyes filling with water as he spoke. Moses didn't say anything after that. A few minutes later, I woke up Cyrus, told Moses goodbye, and we headed home.

On the way home, I thought about Moses. I wasn't sure if it was the pot I'd smoked, but something in me felt sorry for him. Maybe it was the fact that he was somebody's father. Or, maybe it was because somewhere a daughter had a father she could only see every few months. I wasn't sure. What I did know, though, was that after talking to Moses about his daughter, I couldn't help but feel kind of lucky, just knowing I had a father I could see whenever I wanted.

Chapter Twelve

It was DON'T GO IN THE WATER WEEK on TNT, and *Jaws* was showing. On the television, Roy Scheider was sweating beneath the sun, scooping bloody pieces of fish guts over the side of a boat. I took a swig of Zima and glanced over my shoulder at Meridian, who was asleep on Chase's couch curled up in a yellow afghan. Chase combed a hand through his painted black hair and leaned across the table, a smile breaking across his face. "You look like a little slice of Heaven in that skirt," he whispered, his tiny black eyes like loaded dice. I smiled, glanced over my shoulder to make sure Meridian was still sleeping, then unbuttoned the top button of my dress, smirking at him as I fiddled with the button. He took a sip of beer, stood up and walked through the kitchen toward the doorway of his bedroom. When he got to the doorway, he put his finger to his lips and motioned to me to follow him.

When I got into his room, he closed the door behind me, staring down at me for a moment, then leaning in and kissing me on the mouth. While he kissed me, his left hand crawled behind my back and unzipped my black jean skirt.

"Are you crazy?" I whispered, reaching my arm behind my back and grabbing his hand. "For Christ's sake, Meridian's in the next room."

"Let me worry about Meridian." I squirmed out of my skirt while he pulled his silk green shirt over his head. His nipples looked like tiny red eyes staring back at me. He pushed my blouse off my shoulders and it fell to the floor. "I wasn't sure if you'd be up for this," he whispered, his hands worming their way beneath my bra, his hummingbird voice fluttering against my neck. "Meridian said you've been hanging out with some guy who's planning to open a drive-through church. Said you were becoming some kinda holy roller."

"Meridian doesn't know what she's talking about." I reached my hand down and unzipped Chase's jeans. "Anyway, I'm not as holy as she thinks."

Chase smiled. "Good. 'Cause what I got for you, you're not gonna find in any Bible." He slithered out of his white slacks like a snake shedding its skin, and before I knew it, he'd killed the lights, turned me around, and pulled me to the floor. The room was dark except for a blinking red alarm clock and a sky of glow-in-the-dark stars on the ceiling above us. We were on our knees now, like the dogs Meridian and I had seen humping that time, the boy dog's back all bunched up, his red lipstick dangling between his legs, the girl dog squirming in the dirt. Chase pressed his mouth against my neck, pulled down my cotton underwear, and I closed my eyes. I could feel his pecker like a rubbery fish swimming between my legs just before he pushed it in. As it squirmed around inside me, I could feel a pain wriggling between my legs, and I started to feel like my ovaries were crawling into my throat. Chase pushed it deeper a few more times, his body twitched hard, and just like that, it was over.

When we got back into the den, Meridian was still curled up in the yellow afghan on the sofa. I'd always heard that sex made you feel good, but after Chase was done with me, I felt like a pair of teeth had chewed away at my insides. I have to admit, though. It was kind of exciting, knowing that Chase and I had sex while Meridian was sleeping in the next room. She had always made fun of me for being a virgin. But now, the joke was on her, and she didn't have a clue.

The next thing I knew, Chase was bringing Meridian a cup of coffee while she wiped her eyes with her fists. Chase sat down on the sofa next to her, and I pulled the nail polish from my purse and started painting my nails. On TV, Roy Scheider was tossing a silver oxygen tank into the pink mouth of the shark.

Meridian yawned behind her pale hand, blowing on the coffee as she took a sip, her skinny white fingers twisted around the cup handle. "I feel like I crawled out a hog's ass," she yawned.

"What do you expect," Chase told her. "You were sucking back shots of Turkey like they were going outta style. Not to mention that round of Flaming Dr. Pepper's."

I pressed my palm against my knee as I painted my pinkie finger. Out of the corner of my eye, I could see the black veins of Chase's hand rolling under his skin as his finger fondled the tiny brown birthmark on Meridian's thigh. I put the cap on my nail polish and blew on my nails, while on the TV, bloody body parts of the exploded shark fell from the sky like rain.

*   *   *

I got home around ten o'clock, and spent the rest of the night watching TV. Around midnight, I decided to wash a batch of clothes. While I was loading the washer, I noticed something in the back pocket of Daddy's jeans. It was a picture of Iris, the waitress from Nacho Mama's. She was standing under an oak tree in a purple bikini, smiling with her pimpled, makeup-caked face. I thought about hiding the photograph somewhere, but then I remembered what Moses had said, about taking matters into your own hands when God doesn't answer your prayers. I'd spent months praying to God, asking him to save Mama and Daddy's marriage, but no matter how much I prayed, he never answered me. I knew if I wanted to save my parents' marriage, I was going to have to get rid of the picture. As I ripped the picture of Iris into tiny pieces of arms, legs, and eyes, I imagined her strutting around in front of Daddy in that skimpy string bikini, batting her stupid eyelashes, blowing kisses at Daddy, trying to trick him into leaving Mama. When I was done, I stuck the pieces of the photograph in the bottom of the garbage can outside, beneath a pile of rib bones and a half-eaten piece of toast, and then I went back inside.

Chapter Thirteen

When I saw the newspaper the next morning, I felt just like that guy in *The Godfather* must have felt when he opened the newspaper and found a bloody fish wrapped inside. The front page of the *Times Picayune* had a faded, black and white photograph of the kid with the glass bones. A thick black headline above his picture read: ALLEGED CHILD MOLESTER IN ALGIERS DIES AFTER BEATING. The article said the kid had walked around for two days with a blood clot in his brain. It also mentioned his name, CORY RABALAIS. Until then, I hadn't known his last name. All that time, he had been Cory. Just CORY. Nothing else.

For the last few days, I've felt so powerful. But when I realized that we killed that kid, the power I'd felt suddenly turned into a deep black sorrow mixed with bits of fear. I knew Moses had said that some people had to suffer before they could be saved, and that the kid with the glass bones was a sinner, but for some reason, I couldn't help but feel bad for him. I imagined his glass bones, the bruises blooming beneath his pink seashell skin. I thought about praying for him and his family, but I knew if there was a God, he probably wouldn't listen to someone like me.

When I got home, Cyrus was in the yard, working on his car. I could see him bent under the hood as I walked around to the front of the car. He looked up when he saw me, a black smear of oil on his forehead. "Hey Little Sis," he said, wiping his forehead with the back of his hand. "Can you hand me that monkey wrench?"

I walked over to his red toolbox and fished out the monkey wrench.

Cyrus grabbed the wrench and bent down under the hood again. "You saw the paper I guess, huh?"

"Yep."

Cyrus reached his hand down through a nest of black wires, staring at the sky as he felt for a bolt, his teeth clenched, his fingers reading the bolts like braille. He bunched up his face, his arm still stuck in the nest of wires. "Where the Hell's that damn bolt?" He pulled his hand out, yanked a black handkerchief from his back pocket and wiped his hands. "Moses wants to meet up with us tonight. Over at the Paradise Motel."

"I'm worried, Cyrus."

"I know. I still can't believe he's dead. It's like some bad rap video on BET, except it's real."

"What if the cops find out about what we did?"

"Nobody's gonna find out, Hailey." Cyrus grabbed the socket wrench, rooted through the toolbox for a socket, popped the socket onto the end of the wrench and stood up with the wrench in his hand, wiping his forehead with the back of his hand. "Besides, you think the cops are gonna care about some child molester from Algiers?"

"Yeah, but it was wrong, Cyrus. Just 'cause he may or may not have molested some girl."

"I thought you believed in the Bible, Hailey. Doesn't the Bible say that child molesters go to Hell?"

"Yeah, but that's for God to decide, Cyrus. Not us. You can't go around killing everybody you think's a sinner. Beating up people is one thing, but we killed this kid."

"You think I'm glad he's dead, Hailey? I'd do anything to erase what we did. But there's nothing we can do about it now. All we can do at this point is figure out a way to keep ourselves outta jail."

I just stared at Cyrus.

He glanced over at me, the sun creeping across his face. "Look, just go in and get a shower and eat while I fix this, okay. We need to leave here around eight or so."

After I took my shower and ate, I watched TV until it was time to leave. Around eight o'clock, Cyrus and I headed over to the Paradise Motel. On the way there, Cyrus looked the same as he had the night we'd picked up the kid with the glass bones, as if a thought was ticking like a bomb in his head. As he turned onto Elysian Fields, he glanced over at me as he grabbed a brown paper bag between the seat. "What's that mark on your neck?" he asked, pulling an orange from the brown paper bag. "You hurt yourself or something?"

I pulled down the sun visor and noticed what looked like a dark red bruise just above my collarbone.

Cyrus glanced over at me again. "Is that a hickie?"

"I don't think so." I could feel the blood filling my cheeks.

"That's a goddamn hickie, Hailey." Cyrus crumbled the brown paper box in his fist and threw it out the window. "What are you doing with a hickie?"

"I don't know."

"Who gave it to you? I wanna know his name. Right now."

I paused for a moment, trying to think of a name Cyrus wouldn't know, but before I knew what had happened, I opened my mouth and the word "Chase" flew out.

"Chase? Not Chase Haydel?"

"Yeah."

"For Christ's sake, Hailey. He's almost my age."

"I know how old he is."

"That Goddamn pervert." Cyrus balled up his fist and socked the steering wheel. "I swear, I'm gonna beat the Jesus outta that boy."

"Leave him alone, Cyrus. It's none of your business."

"None of my business? My little sister getting some hickie from a nineteen year old man's none of my business?"

"No, it's not. I can get a hickie from whoever I want. Anyway, you can't go around socking everybody in the world you don't like. You don't see Daddy slugging every person that pisses him off."

"Yeah, Daddy." Cyrus laughed under his breath. "Some role model he turned out to be. Don't even get me started on him."

"Why do you hate him so much, anyway?"

"I don't hate him." Cyrus peeled the orange, throwing pieces of orange skin out the window as he peeled each sliver off. He threw the last piece of orange peel out the window, and took another bite. "I've just had it with him dragging our name though the dirt. That's all."

"You know, Mama's not exactly a saint."

"What's that supposed to mean?"

"Verma said Mama cheated on Daddy. When they first got married."

"Cheated on Daddy? Mama?"

"It's true. Verma said it happened a long time ago. And that Daddy had forgiven her for it."

"I don't believe that for a second."

"Why would Verma lie?"

"I dunno." Cyrus was picking at a dirty band-aid on his arm. He peeled the Band-Aid back and started picking at a bloody scab. "She must be mistaken, that's all."

"I don't think so."

"You're sure? She said *Mama* cheated on *Daddy*?"

"Positive. That's why I couldn't understand why you were so pissed off at Daddy all the time. It's not like he's the only one doing it. And if Mama did it first . . . "

"What do you mean, Daddy's not the only one doing it?"

"Well, you know, cause Daddy's cheating on Mama too."

Cyrus turned his eyes on me. "Who told you that?"

"No one told me."

"I mean it, Hailey. Who told you?"

"No one told me, Cyrus. I figured it out for myself. I'm not stupid, you know."

"Son-of-a-bitch."

"What? What's wrong?"

"That's not something you should know, Hailey," he said, rubbing his forehead with a pale hand. His voice grew soft. "You're just a goddamn kid. You supposed to be having fun. Doing what kids do. Not worrying about whether your stupid parents are screwing around on one another."

"I know but . . . "

"This family. I swear to God, it's like we're all drowning in quicksand or something. We're up to our eyes in it, all of us. And we don't even know it."

"I know, Cyrus. But you can't protect me from everything, you know."

"This family's poisonous, Hailey. The only way you're gonna make anything of your life is to get as far away from us as you can. Just promise me you're gonna go away to college when you graduate. Please, Hailey. Just promise me that."

"I promise, Cyrus. I promise."

*   *   *

When we got to the motel, the parking lot was empty, except for a green dumpster swarming with flies. The hotel sign was strung with Christmas lights. In the swimming pool beneath the sign, a white crescent moon bobbed against the ripple of beer cans.

Moses's green Omni rattled into the parking lot around five after ten. He pulled up next to Cyrus's Hyundai and got out, his lips shiny with chicken grease. He didn't have a shirt on. It was the first time I'd seen him without a shirt. As he drifted into the light, I could see a tattoo on his chest. It was the torso of Jesus, the chest and two arms outstretched against a plank of wood, like a cross, and each of Moses's nipples was a nail hole in Jesus' wrist.

"I take it both of you seen the write up in the *Picayune* this morning," Moses said to us, sucking on a chicken wing, his spicy breath floating in the black air.

"Yeah," Cyrus told him. "You think we need to be worried?"

Moses swatted a gnat from his neck, grabbed a can of Red Bull from the hood of his green Omni and took a swig. "The cops ain't stupid. Pretty soon, they gonna be on us like ticks." He threw the chicken wing into a clump of dead weeds, licked his shiny lips, then wiped his mouth with a dirty hand. "Just make sure the two of ya got your stories straight."

"Yeah. I was thinking of that."

"The cops, they trained to look for inconsistencies. Anything that don't fit. Stories that don't match up. Time lines that are all outta whack. That sorta thing. They ain't got no evidence to link us to the scene. So, all you gotta do is keep your story straight, and you're home free. You ain't told nobody else about what happened, have you?"

"Nope." Cyrus rubbed his forehead with a sweaty hand. "Haven't breathed a word."

"Good." Moses stared at him through the black worm holes of his eyes. "Just keep that trap of yours shut and everything'll work out fine." He rubbed his pot belly, wiping a handprint of chicken grease off his pants, then picked a piece of chicken from his teeth with a dirty fingernail. "And stay away from the old bank," he said, biting his lip. "Place'll be swarming with pigs fore too long."

"What are you gonna do?" Cyrus asked.

"Nothing I can do now but wait. See what the cops turn up." Moses grinned. "I never figured we'd kill that kid. Not in a million years."

"I know." Cyrus told him. "I still can't believe it."

Moses squeezed the Red Bull can until it crackled in his fist and threw it in a nearby ditch. "Hell, if I'd known how bad off he was, I'd grabbed them brass knuckles from you and finished the job myself."

Cyrus paused for a moment. "You want me to call you?" he asked, "if I hear anything?"

"Naw. Stay off the phone. Those pigs get suspicious enough, they'll start tapping the phone lines too."

When Moses and Cyrus were finished talking, Cyrus and I got back in the car. As we pulled out of the parking lot, I watched Moses disappear in the side mirror. Piece by piece, the hotel faded into the swirling dust, until there was nothing left, except the pink neon word VACANCY blinking against the black sky.

Chapter Fourteen

Trashy Diva was a fancy dress shop in the French Quarter. Lorelei Evans's annual costume party was a week away, and I'd decided to go as Medusa, so Mama had brought me to Trashy Diva to get a dress. The day before, she'd even bought some rubber snakes and pinned them to barrettes for me to put in my hair.

"This place is expensive," I said, staring at myself in a full-length mirror.

"So what."

"Don't you think Daddy's gonna be mad if we buy a dress from here?"

"Yeah well, I'm sick of hording all my money like I'm poverty-stricken," Mama said, fixing her hair in the mirror. "This is a special occasion, and it calls for an expensive dress."

I stared into the mirror, thinking about what color eye shadow I was going to wear. As I tilted my head, I noticed a small white-head near the corner of my nose. "Did Daddy ever take you to parties when you were dating?" I asked, scratching the white-head with a red paint-flaked fingernail.

Mama grabbed a white dress with a heart-shaped bodice and held it up in front of me. "Not too many," she said, tilting her head to one side. "I always wanted to go to a Mardi Gras Ball, but after I married your daddy we couldn't afford it. My momma used to take me to the Endymion Ball when I was a little girl, and I loved it. They used to serve filet mignon and fancy champagne. You felt like you were royalty when you were there." Mama stared at me in the mirror for a moment. "Are you sure the waist isn't too tight?"

I held my arms up while Mama pinched the material around the waist of the dress.

"If you'd like, I can take you to Paris Parker Friday to get your hair done."

"Are you sure? I can just do it myself."

"We can't have you going to some costume party looking like a hooligan. I'll take you over there on Friday afternoon. After you get home from school. We can make a day of it."

"Thanks."

"You're welcome." Mama stood behind me in the mirror, tucking a strand of my hair behind my ear. "Your daddy said you're going with Jay to the party, huh?"

"Yeah. We're going as friends."

"Friends? Well, you just make sure he doesn't get too friendly. You don't need some boy pawing on you all night. Especially not in a fancy dress like this."

"We're just friends."

"Un, huh. Well, when Jay sees you in this dress, that boy's eyes are gonna pop clean out his head."

"Yeah, right."

"I'm serious. Look at yourself in the mirror." Mama ran a hand along the curve of my hip. "Look at these hips. Women would give their right arm for hips like these." She cupped my waist with her hand. "And would you look at this tiny little waist. You've got a perfect hourglass figure if I've ever seen one. Just be sure to keep that beautiful body of yours in that dress. After all, God designed sex for procreation, not recreation."

We decided on the blue dress, and Mama went and paid for it while I changed back into my regular clothes. As I was tying my shoes, I could hear her arguing with the owner about the fact that Mama's credit card had been declined. "Do you know what my maiden name is?" Mama yelled. "My father was Henry Godchaux for God's sake."

In the end, the lady didn't seem to care who Mama's father was, and Mama was forced to write a check for the dress. On the way home, she told me the check she'd given the lady wasn't worth the paper it was written on, and that she hoped it bounced all the way to the bank.

*　　*　　*

Later that day, while Cyrus was under his car changing the oil, I noticed Uncle Errol's shiny yellow Hummer outside. As I walked outside, I saw Cyrus crawling out from under his car.

"Your daddy here?" Uncle Errol asked, taking off his silver mirrored sunglasses, exposing a dull, yellow-green bruise around his eye. He placed a brown briefcase on the shiny yellow hood of his Hummer.

"What you want?" Cyrus asked, wiping a line of grease from his forehead with a sweaty hand.

"Got some papers for your Daddy to sign." Uncle Errol opened the brown briefcase, placed his sunglasses on the yellow hood of the Hummer.

"He's not here," Cyrus said.

"Well." Uncle Errol licked his fingers as he thumbed through a stack of papers in his briefcase. "I need to leave these here for him." His movements were robot-like. If you sliced him open, you'd probably find machine guts in his insides. I imagined a clump of burned-out wires instead of an intestine, a tiny little hard drive instead of a brain. "Here it is," he said, pulling a yellow paper from the briefcase. He held the paper out and Cyrus snatched it from his hand.

Cyrus glanced down at the paper, his black hair flickering in the sun. "What's this?"

"An eviction notice. Your daddy's got three months to move out." Uncle Errol glanced up at Cyrus, his face like a mask. "Before I get the law involved." He closed the briefcase, walked over to the passenger's side, put the briefcase in his car, then walked back toward the front of the car, where Cyrus and I were standing. He pulled a white silk monogrammed handkerchief from his pants pocket and blotted his forehead with it. "Tell your daddy if he's got any questions to call me at my office."

Cyrus looked up from the paper and turned his eyes on Uncle Errol. "You got some nerve bringing this over here like this."

"Look Cyrus, I cut your daddy a lot of slack on this. Us being family and all. But he's got to realize . . . "

"Family?" Cyrus hissed. "You're about to throw your own sister out of her house for Christ's sake. Not to mention her children. You're not family, Errol. You're a goddamned amoeba. That's what you are." Cyrus ripped the paper into pieces and tossed them into the air, the bits of paper floating to the ground like the feathers of a shot bird.

Uncle Errol stared at Cyrus through his murky brown eyes. "You'd been better off if you hadn't done that, Cyrus."

"We'd be better off if someone put you out of your misery."

"Yeah, well, maybe so, but that ain't gonna change the fact that your daddy ain't paid his bills."

"You know he's outta work, Errol."

"Yeah. And he's been outta work for nearly six months now. The world don't stop spinning for your daddy, Cyrus."

"We never asked for it to stop spinning. All we asked for was a little damn consideration. That's all."

"I feel terrible for everything your momma had to go through. Believe me I do. Having a miscarriage and all. And I been praying for her. I pray for her every night. Every single night."

"You can keep your prayers, Errol. We don't want 'em. As you can see, they aren't doing us much good around here anyhow."

"You're not so far gone that you stopped believing in Jesus, are you?"

"Stopped believing? Hell, I never started believing."

"Just 'cause your family's down on their luck don't give you a reason to go doubting your faith. Jesus is with you all the time. You know that. Even when you're in the Valley of Darkness. Like the scripture says. He's even with you then. When you're at your worst."

Cyrus held his hands out, his white palms facing the sky as he glanced around the yard. "Where's Jesus, Errol? Huh? You see Jesus anywhere?"

"I'm not gonna stand here and let you mock my faith, Cyrus."

"You don't see him anywhere? Do you? Do you, Errol? You wanna know why? 'Cause Jesus wouldn't be caught dead in this stinking place. That's why."

"You got problems, Cyrus." Uncle Errol tapped his finger against the side of his skull, the words turning in the tiny little hard drive in his head. "Your head's not screwed on right. These problems got your head all messed up."

"My head's working just fine. And this conversation's over. Go on." Cyrus spit a wad of phlegm into the dirt, wiped his mouth with the back of his hand. "Get outta here," he hissed. "Before I give you a fresh black eye to match the one you got."

Uncle Errol wiped the sweat from his forehead with his silk handkerchief, turned around and walked to the driver's side of his Hummer. "Just tell your daddy I stopped by," he said, climbing into the car and starting the engine. He turned the Hummer around, shoved the car in drive, and headed down the driveway.

*   *   *

"Does it hurt?" I asked Chase, my finger tracing a blue bruise on his cheek.

Chase turned onto Chef Menteur, glancing over at me and grinning. "Just when I smile."

"I can't believe you're not mad."

"Mad about what?"

"Mad that my stupid goon of a brother slugged you in the face."

"I don't mind. I like fighting."

I smiled. "It doesn't look to me like you did much fighting."

"I gotta a few good licks in. Before he punched my lights out."

"I don't know who the Hell he thinks he is. Butting into my business like that."

"You can't really blame him, Hailey. If you were my sister, I wouldn't want you hanging out with me either."

Chase turned onto the gravel road that led to The Dead Goat. He drove down the road, parked next to an abandoned old car near the weedy edge of the canal and killed the engine. He grabbed a Zima from the ice chest behind his seat, took a swig, then began tracing a little red scar on my knee with his veiny hand.

"So," I said, "you never did tell me why you're so obsessed with scars."

"I'm not obsessed. I just like 'em, that's all."

"What's there to like about a scar?"

"I dunno." Chase massaged his earlobe with a manicured finger. "These days, it seems like everybody's so damn obsessed with looking perfect. They whiten their teeth, shoot Botox into their foreheads. I guess I like 'em 'cause they prove we're not so damn perfect after all, you know. Plus, they kinda tell a story if you think about it. Whenever I see a scar, I'm always wondering how the person got it." He took a swig of beer as he stared out the window at an orange-red sun bleeding through a piece of sheet metal. "When I was a kid, my grandmother used to work for this funeral parlor. I used to go there with her sometime, when my parents were on one of their trips. Anyway, sometimes, when she was dressing up the body, just to kill time really, she'd find some scar, and we'd play this game where we'd make up stories about how the person got it. My grandmother could make up the best damn stories."

Chase stared out the window at an old junked Cadillac that looked like it had been stripped and abandoned. All the tires had been taken off and weeds were growing from under the dented hood. He watched a rat scurry into a rusted hole in the Cadillac's fender, then sucked what was left of the Zima from the bottle and chucked it out the window.

"That's enough talking for now." He slid across the seat and climbed on top of me, kissing me on my neck as his hand unbuttoned my blouse. He reached down the side of the seat and adjusted it so that I was lying flat on my back. As his hand crawled under my blouse, I stared out the window of the Firebird, watching as an orange-red sun sank into the murky brown water of the canal.

Chapter Fifteen

By the time Cyrus and I left for the hospital, dusk had wormed its way through the guts of the trees, choking off the last little bits of light. After her appointment on Friday, the doctor had decided to admit Verma to the hospital. He said the diabetes had eaten up the veins in her legs. Before the miscarriage, when Mama used to work at the hospital, she'd tell us about the diabetes patients, how when the disease ate up the veins in their feet, their toes turned black and fell off. We were nearly halfway to Mercy Hospital before Cyrus told me that the doctor had cut off Verma's right leg. I thought about how the preacher had laid hands on Verma's leg, how the congregation had prayed to God that he'd spare it, how once again, God had ignored our prayers.

"You still mad at me?" Cyrus asked, taking a bite of a ham sandwich.

"Yes, I'm still mad at you. I can't believe you punched Chase."

"Punched him?" Cyrus wiped a Hitler moustache of mayonnaise from his lip. "He's lucky that's all I did. I should of called the cops and had his ass thrown in jail."

"All he did was give me a hickey, Cyrus. Hasn't a girl ever given you a hickey before?"

"Sure. I've gotten my share of hickeys, but I've never given one to a sixteen-year-old girl." Cyrus glanced in the rearview mirror, picking a piece of bread from his teeth. "That kid's a slug, Hailey. You don't need to be hanging out with someone like that."

"I can hang out with anyone I want to hang out with, Cyrus. I don't know why you feel the need to butt into my life so much."

" 'Cause I'm your brother, that's why. I'm supposed to protect you from people like that."

"Yeah, well. I don't need you to protect me."

"So what?" Cyrus took another bite of the ham sandwich. "You expect me to let you hang out with scum like that? You expect me just to sit back and do nothing?"

"Chase is not scum, Cyrus. I like him. He treats me nice. Anyway, you don't even know him."

"He's a pervert, Hailey. Plain and simple. And I'm not letting some pervert screw around with my little sister. If that makes me an asshole, then so be it."

We didn't say anything after that. When we got to the hospital, I climbed out of the Hyundai. Cyrus said he'd wait for me in the parking lot. I wondered why he didn't want to come in, but I was too mad at him to even ask. Mama had said that Verma was in room 224, so when I got inside the hospital, I went to the elevator and made my way to the second floor. When I found Verma's room, I knocked on the door. I didn't hear anyone answer, so I opened the door and peeked my head in. Verma was lying in the bed, her head propped on two pillows that looked like two white clouds. Her face was flat, her lips bunched up in her mouth.

"Hailey," she wheezed, her eyebrows cocked.

I walked over to a chair that was next to Verma's bed. A bed pan filled with urine was on the table next to me. It looked like a smiling silver mouth.

As I sat down, the door opened, and a woman in white walked in, wheeling a cart of food. "It's lunchtime, Mrs. Williams." The lady wheeled the cart to the foot of the bed and left.

As she was leaving, I thanked her and pushed the cart closer to Verma. "You ready to eat?" I asked. I couldn't help but stare at the empty white space where Verma's leg had been.

Verma motioned to me with her good eye closed, only the dead eye staring back at me. I picked up the fork and stabbed it into a stringy piece of roast beef and put the fork to her mouth. Her lips cracked open, and I guided the fork into her mouth. She swallowed all of what was on the fork, except for a small piece of roast beef that dribbled down her chin. "How you feeling?" I asked, wiping her chin with the napkin.

Her lips rolled around in her mouth for a second while she chewed the roast beef. "Those rotten bastards took my leg," she said, swallowing the bite of roast beef. She put the straw between her teeth and sucked the water into the tight brown fist of her mouth. Her lips rolled around in her mouth as she sucked on the straw.

I looked on the table next to me and saw the artificial leg. It was beige and smooth like a mannequin's leg with little metal hinges at the knee and ankle.

"Are you feeling okay?"

"I'm fine. For a one-legged old woman I spose." She rubbed her forehead with an ashy brown hand. "Gonna have to plug some plastic leg into my hip to get around now," she said, talking between sips. "Got a bum hip. Couldn't hear a freight train barreling toward me with these ears I got. Now this diabetes comes along and takes my leg. But, shit, these doctors ain't killed me yet."

"Are you having any pain?"

"Nope. They got me all hopped up on pain meds. For when the pain in my ghost foot starts."

When Mama had worked in the hospital, she had told me that amputees sometimes could feel their missing limb years after it had been cut off. They called it phantom pain.

"Can you believe that?" Verma chewed each word and handed the cup back to me. "Pain in my ghost foot? As if I the one I got ain't hurting enough."

I thought about the leg the doctor had chopped off, wondering what they had done with it, wondering if the leg had a memory, if it somehow still remembered the body it had been stuck to. I imagined the black toes wiggling after the doctor cut it off, like the chickens I'd seen at my grandfather's house in the country, hopping around the yard after their heads had been lopped off.

I smiled at Verma. "Mama said your sister's coming to bring you home tomorrow."

"Yeah. She's gonna bring me back to the house and stay with me for a few days. Says she's gonna take me to Galatoire's. Once I'm feeling better."

Galatoire's was one of the most expensive restaurants in New Orleans, and once a month, Verma's sister took her there to eat.

"She'll probably take me over to Wal-Mart too. I need to get a few things. That reminds me. Be sure to tell your daddy that I haven't forgot about that job interview. Soon as I get outta this hospital, I'm gonna call that friend of mine and see if I can't get him another interview."

I smiled. "You don't give up, do you?"

"No Ma'am. I'm gonna get that daddy of yours a job if it kills me. You'll see."

"Alright, I'll tell him, but try to get some rest all right?"

I fed Verma the rest of her dinner. All that was left was a pile of bright green string beans and a yellow sliver of apple pie. After she'd finished, I told her I'd see her when she got home, and I kissed her on the cheek and left.

I went down to the gift shop and got a bouquet of white lilies. I figured I'd go and see Mr. Guidry, since I was already at the hospital. After I bought the flowers, I walked up to his room, but when I got there, the door was closed. I knocked, but no one answered. When I opened the door, I noticed that Mr. Guidry's bed was empty, so I went down to the nurse's station and asked where he was. One of the nurses pulled me aside and told me he'd passed away on Wednesday. I couldn't believe it. I'd just seen him a week or so ago. I could feel my eyes filling with tears. I didn't want some stupid nurse to see me crying, so I turned around and headed for the elevator. When I got down to the first floor parking lot, I noticed a green dumpster. I threw the bouquet of lilies into the dumpster and knelt down on the ground, crying. *Why had God let someone so nice die?* I was so mad at God for taking Mr. Guidry. I sat there crying for a few minutes, but I knew Cyrus was waiting for me, so I wiped my eyes with the sleeve of my blouse and headed across the street toward his car.

*   *   *

That night, I dreamed I was standing in a field of purple flowers. In the dream, my organs were rotting inside my body. My heart and my lungs felt like rotten meat, and each breath I took buzzed in my chest like a swarm of dirty flies. For some reason, Jesus was standing next to me. He was wearing a tuxedo, and I was dressed in a white straightjacket. My fists were clenched, and when Jesus opened them, I could see bloody nail holes in my wrists. When the dream ended, Jesus was flying up to Heaven, and I was standing in the field all alone, like a fallen white angel with its wings chopped off.

Chapter Sixeen

The words RAT BASTARD had been carved into the chipped, orange paint on the passenger side door of Daddy's Nova, and Daddy was next to the car, leaning down on one knee in the yard, his finger pressed against a bloody cut in the corner of his mouth while Cyrus stood over him, his left hand balled into a fist.

"If it wasn't somebody you owed money," Cyrus asked, "then who did it?"

Daddy kept his hand pressed against the bloody cut in the corner of his mouth. "There's a whole slew of people who think I'm a rat bastard, Son. You know that. You really expect me to narrow down a list that long to one or two people?"

"Everything's a goddamn joke with you," Cyrus hissed. "We both know who it was. Just say it. It was that silly little waitress from Nacho Mama's. Why don't you just admit it?" Cyrus unballed his fist and stood there waiting for Daddy to answer. But Daddy didn't say a word. He only stared down at the ground, at a fresh drop of blood in the dirt.

"You're pathetic." Cyrus spit a peppermint at Daddy and walked over to his Hyundai and climbed in. He cranked the engine, yanked it into drive and peeled out of the yard, a white cloud of dust hovering in the air as he left.

When I walked over to Daddy, he was sitting in the dirt, his thick black-rimmed glasses cracked, a map of dirt on his forehead. I asked him if he was all right, pulled his red handkerchief from his coat pocket, and pressed it against the line of blood in the corner of his mouth. He held the handkerchief against his lip with one hand and pulled his nicotine inhaler from his shirt pocket.

"Damn," he said, taking a puff off the inhaler between words. "That brother of yours packs one Hell of a punch."

I took his cracked eyeglasses and put them in my pocket. "I don't know what's gotten into Cyrus." I brushed the dusted bits of gravel off the leather collar of his coat.

"Don't get the red-ass at your brother, Hailey. He's got reasons for what he did."

"Don't make excuses for him, Daddy." I tucked a long curled strand of hair behind his ear. "There isn't a reason in the world for anybody to go slugging their own father."

A smirk squirmed in the corner of Daddy's mouth. "Hell, I've spent most of my life giving that boy reasons to slug me." He pressed his tongue against his cheek, his finger tracing a line of blood in the corner of his mouth. "Tell you the truth," he said, wetting his finger with his tongue and wiping a smear of blood from his two front teeth. "I'm surprised it didn't happen sooner."

I could hear Daddy's bones creak as I helped him to his feet. As I walked him toward the porch, I saw Mama standing in the doorway.

"Are you two finished beating each other to death?" she asked, handing me a bottle of peroxide and a cotton ball.

"Whatcha think the neighbors are gonna think, when they see two grown men fist fighting in the yard? Middle class people don't act like this."

"Who cares what the neighbors think?" I sat Daddy down on the couch and knelt down on one knee, blotting his lip with the peroxide-soaked cotton ball. "Can't you see Daddy's hurt?"

"He's not hurt. Stop doting over your father and go to your room."

"I'm helping him."

"He doesn't need your help. Now do like I said. Go to your room."

Mama reached for my arm, and I jerked it away. "Go to your room now, Hailey. Your daddy can take care of himself."

"It's okay, Hailey," Daddy said, holding the cotton ball against the bloody cut in the corner of his mouth. "I'm fine. Go ahead and go to your room. Like your momma said."

Mama reached down and grabbed my arm and pulled me to my feet. "I said go, Hailey."

"You know," I said, jerking Mama's arm away. "You're not so perfect."

"I mean it, Hailey. Go to your room now. I'm not gonna say it again."

"Verma told me what you did. About how you cheated on Daddy after you first got married."

I stood there and stared at her, but I didn't move. Mama grabbed me by the arm and marched me into my room. "I don't know what in the Hell's gotten into you, Hailey," she said, turning me loose when we got into my bedroom. "But I've had it with you tonight."

"You act like you're so much better than everybody. I guess you're not so perfect after all, huh?"

"Who said I was perfect? Anyway, that was a long time ago. Your daddy's forgiven me for that."

"I don't know who's worse. You or Daddy."

"That's a real nice thing to say about your parents."

"You two aren't parents. Parents help their kids. They don't abandon them. You and Daddy are so busy screwing up your own lives, you forgot all about Cyrus and me. Where are you and Daddy when I got problems? Huh? Where are you when I got something I need to talk about? All we ever talk about is that dead baby, about how miserable your life is, about how your life never worked out the way you wanted it to. What about me? I have a life too you know."

"Poor, little Hailey. Life's so difficult. Having to worry about what you're gonna wear tomorrow or what boy you're gonna kiss next. How do you ever find the time?"

"My problems are important too."

"You should be glad I cheated on Daddy. Now you've got one more reason to complain to everybody about how terrible your life is." Mama walked over to the doorway and glanced back at me. "Go ahead and blame me and your daddy for your miserable life if you like. I don't care one way or another."

*　　*　　*

That night I went in the garage and found an old piece of cardboard and duct-taped it to the passenger side door of Daddy's Nova, to cover the words RAT BASTARD. When I got back inside, I fixed Daddy a Hungry Man dinner and brought him a Coke. When I was done, I called Chase. I left a few messages on his cell phone, but he didn't return my calls. I felt like that woman from *Fatal Attraction*, you know the one I'm talking about, that crazy blonde with the slit wrists who sat in her room flipping the light switch on and off as if a fuse had come loose in her brain. I started thinking about hurting myself to get Chase's attention, putting myself in the hospital so he'd come and visit me. I thought about taking a handful of Mama's sleeping pills. I imagined myself like Snow White, a smiling corpse lying under a glass sky, Chase smiling over me with his little red doll's mouth, waking me from my dead sleep with one of his sloppy little kisses.

Chapter Seventeen

The front of the old abandoned warehouse where they held the dog fights was speckled with rusted bullet holes. The windows of the building had been punched out, and shards of glass flickered in the dirt like diamonds. Inside, people, mostly guys, were gathered in a circle, most of them cheering, waving sweaty wads of dollar bills wound with rubber bands, drinking beer. As we got closer, I saw Moses smile at us through the crowd.

"Hey Chief." Moses said, sucking on a red popsickle. He high-fived Cyrus, glancing over at me, a pitbull with a spiked collar next to him sprawled out on the cement, panting with its pink tongue. "Hey, Miss Hailey. Did you meet Hitler?"

"He looks bigger than usual," Cyrus said.

Moses leaned down and scratched the pitbull behind its white ear. "Yeah. I've been feeding him like a hog for months, trying to beef 'em up for the big fight. He's put on almost two pounds in the last week."

"What do you feed him?" Cyrus asked. "Raw meat?"

Moses smiled. "Catholics mostly."

Silas laughed and said something, but his words drowned beneath the cheering of the crowd and the ringing of a bell. The cheering grew louder and louder until the mass of people slowly parted, revealing a muscular bald kid in overalls with thick arms carrying a grey pitbull. The dog was panting furiously, its tongue hanging out the side of its mouth. Across from us, a boy wearing jeans with missing knees and a fake tuxedo shirt was standing next to a fat man with a pencil behind his ear. The fat man pulled out a wad of money, licking his fingers as he counted off the bills and laid them in the boy's hand. There were two lines of duct tape near each corner of the pit. Cyrus said these were called scratch lines. He said the dogs had to cross these lines before they could attack each other.

"I think it's time," Moses said. As the fat man with the pencil behind his ear rang a bell, Moses moved through the clutter of people, toward the pit, leading Hitler by the collar. When he got to the center of the pit, he moved to the far corner. Standing in the other corner was a yellow haired kid holding a chocolate colored pitbull by the collar. When the second bell rang, Moses and the boy released the dogs. The pitbulls lunged toward each other, rising up on their hind legs as they met, their front paws raised, their teeth biting the air. With a quick turn of his head, the chocolate colored dog caught Hitler on the ear and locked his jaw there, his back arched, the bony curves of his ribs protruding through his thin brown skin. Somehow, though, Hitler squirmed loose. For a moment, the two dogs circled one another, lunging toward each other again as the crowd cheered. As Hitler leaped forward, the chocolate pitbull caught him again, this time on the back. Hitler wrestled loose again, but as he jerked his muscular black neck, the other dog caught him on the throat. You could hear the dog's toenails scratching against the pavement as he pushed Hitler backward, toward the edge of the pit. When Hitler had reached the edge of the pit, the fat man with the pencil behind his ear rang the bell again. And just like that, the whole thing was over.

Moses grabbed Hitler by the collar and guided him away from the pit, walking him through the clutter of cheering boys while the fat man with the pencil behind his ear handed the boy a wad of cash. Moses looked over his shoulder and saw the kid smiling over at him, waving a fan of hundred dollar bills.

"Boy's got some set of balls," Moses mumbled, unscrewing a brown bottle of peroxide. "Waving his winnings at me like that." Moses soaked the cotton ball with peroxide and dabbed the cotton ball against the cut on Hitler's neck. While he held the cotton ball on the cut, I heard him whisper something into Hitler's ear. You could tell he loved that dog, the way he nuzzled his face in the dog's ear, petting it with long, soft strokes, dabbing peroxide anywhere he saw blood.

As he knelt down, dabbing peroxide on the cut on Hitler's neck, a skinny man with a brown ponytail walked over. He was wearing a white t-shirt and blue jeans, and he had a small patch of yellow hair atop his head.

"Hey Moses," the man said.

Moses glanced up and smiled, exposing his dirty yellow teeth "Smiley. My man." Moses put down the brown bottle of peroxide and reached up to shake the man's hand. "How you been?"

"Can't complain, I guess," the man said, smiling down at Moses.

Moses glanced up at the man as he poured peroxide onto a cotton ball. "So whatcha been up to? You still working the same gig? Over in Gretna?"

"Nah." The man rubbed his small pot belly as he spoke. "They got me working over in this neck of the woods now."

"Oh yeah? What they got you doing?"

"Surveillance mostly. Busting up drug rings. That kinda thing."

Moses wiped a long white string of drool from Hitler's mouth. "They promote you to detective yet?"

The man smiled. "Nah. Just a lowly informant. That's all."

"Hell, I'm glad you're back," Moses told him. "I could use a second pair of ears."

"Oh yeah? You not getting yourself into any trouble are you?"

Moses smiled. "You know me. I don't go looking for it. It just seems to find me somehow. I'd love to pick ya brain sometime."

"Sure. Let's get together."

"Anything happening on the Rabalais Case I should know about?"

The man leaned in. "The department's been co-operating with the precinct over in Algiers. They got a list of local people they plan to interrogate. But that's all I know at this point." He glanced over his shoulder, then back at Moses. "Let's get together sometime and talk about it. Somewhere a little more private." The crowd began to cheer, and the man winced. "I'm heading out. It was good seeing you, Moses. Give me a call sometime. Maybe we can grab a beer or something."

"Sure thing, Smiley," Moses said, shaking the man's hand. "Take it easy."

Chapter Eighteen

The River Shack Tavern was on River Road, just down the street from St. Agnes Church and a brand new Piccadilly Cafeteria. After the costume party, Chase asked me and Meridian if we wanted to go out drinking. Jay had a ten o'clock curfew, so Chase dropped him off first. Chase said he knew the bartender, and that they wouldn't card us. Me and Meridian agreed to keep our costumes on for fun, so I was still wearing my Medusa outfit. Meridian had gone to the party as a sexy nun. The outfit was black leather, and it was cut low on her chest so you could see her fake boobs. She was wearing a nun's habit, black fingernail polish, black lipstick, black spiked heels, and a black cross around her neck.

All along the bar were stools, each with a different mannequin's leg. There was one with a pink and black garter belt wrapped around the thigh, another with black fish-net stockings, and another with red thigh-highs. The woman behind the bar had her hair in a ponytail with a wall of black bangs hiding her forehead. Her yellow t-shirt strangled her chest so that her boobs looked like two cantaloupes jammed together. A gold crucifix dangled from a chain, sandwiched between the cantaloupes. She had skin the color of pancake batter and a tattoo of a white magnolia on her right cantaloupe.

Meridian and I grabbed a table near the wall while Chase ordered us drinks. There were about twenty or so other people there. No one I really recognized to tell you the truth. As I looked around the room, I noticed that each table had some kind of weird ashtray. The ashtray on our table was a frog with a big silver mouth.

A few minutes later, Chase came over to the table and sat down.

"This place is a stinking hole in the wall," Meridian snapped, capping her lipstick and putting it back in her purse.

Chase smiled at me. "She's so easy to please, isn't she?"

I smiled back at Chase.

"What they got on the jukebox?" Meridian asked.

"Mostly classic rock," Chase told her. "And some new stuff. My Chemical Romance, Marilyn Manson. Stuff like that."

"Ooh. I love Marilyn Manson." Meridian turned to Chase. "You got some money for me?"

Chase dug into his pockets, pulled out two wrinkled dollar bills, and handed them to Meridian.

"Any requests?" Meridian asked, fanning herself with the dollar bills.

"Nope," Chase said.

As Meridian walked toward the jukebox, Chase turned his eyes on me. "I can't stand Marilyn Manson." He pulled the little hand grenade lighter from his pocket and lit a cigarette. "You wanna smoke?" Chase handed me a Pall Mall and I stuck it in my mouth. As he lit the cigarette, he smiled back at me. "Whatcha think?" he said, his hand creeping under the table toward my thigh. "Wanna head on over to my place for a nightcap?"

I smiled back at him, glancing over at the jukebox where Meridian was standing, her skinny white hand fiddling with the habit of the nun costume as she looked for a song.

"What about Meridian?"

"What about her?" Chase smiled, his hand rubbing my thigh.

As I stared at him, his hand crept between my thighs. When he did this, I squeezed my hips together, so that he couldn't get his hand out. When Meridian turned around and started to walk toward our table, I unsqueezed my thighs, expecting Chase to move his hand. But he didn't. Instead, he kept it right where it was, stuck between my thighs.

"Did you find something?" Chase asked Meridian as she sat down.

"All they had was 'The Dope Show'."

By this time, the bartender was walking over to our table with a tray of frosted mugs and a pitcher of Purple Haze. She handed the pitcher to Chase and gave us each a frosted mug. "Here you go, Baby," she said, smiling over at Chase. "Want me to start a tab for you?"

"Sure thing, Colleen." Chase smiled back at her as he poured Meridian a beer.

As Colleen walked off, Meridian turned her eyes on Chase. "You get a good look?"

"What? At Colleen?" Chase smiled. "Come on, Meridian." He took a sip of Purple Haze.

"Woman needs to find herself a gold miner," Meridian hissed. "To dig that cross out from between those mountains she calls tits."

Chase smiled, glancing over at me. "She's in rare form tonight."

By now, his other hand was drifting across my knee. I have to admit, it was kind of exciting. Chase stroking my leg right under Meridian's nose. Knowing that Meridian didn't have a clue.

"I gotta piss like a race horse," Meridian said. "Wanna take a trip with me to the Little Girl's Room, Hailey?"

The bathroom was at the back of the bar. Inside, there was a sink filled with dirty water. Above it, a mirror smudged with fingerprints. There was a single toilet in the corner of the room. The chrome toilet seat was sprinkled with urine, the floor around it strewn with wet pieces of toilet paper.

"Why are you so pissy tonight?" I asked, watching as Meridian puckered in the smudged mirror, circling her lips with black lipstick.

"I dunno. Just in a bad mood, I guess," Meridian wiped a smudge of lipstick from the corner of her mouth with a long black fingernail.

"Anything I can do?" I really didn't care, but I figured I'd ask anyway.

"I missed my period. That's all."

"That's all? My God, Meridian. What are you going to do?"

Meridian tucked a strand of hair behind her ear. "I ain't exactly got a plan yet."

"How late are you?"

"Three weeks."

"Jesus. Is it Chase's?"

"Hell if I know."

"Who else have you been with?"

"Two or three other guys." She smiled at me in the mirror with her fat black collagen lips. "Give or take a few."

"This isn't funny, Meridian."

"I know it's not funny, Hailey. How do you think I feel? I'm the one's gonna have to pay for it."

"Pay for what? An abortion?"

"Yeah an abortion," Meridian said, pulling a bottle of poison from her purse. "What you think? I'm gonna keep it?"

"I don't know. Maybe."

"You must be crazy if you think I'm gonna lug some stupid baby around for nine months." She sprayed a puff of perfume between her freckled boobs. "Maybe I'll get lucky, and somebody'll push me down a flight of steps."

"I thought you were on the pill."

Meridian pulled a tube of mascara from her purse. "I am," she said, curling her eyelashes with the mascara brush. "But nothing's 100%."

"Does Chase know?"

"No. And I don't want him to know either. It's none of his damn business."

"None of his business? But what if it's his, Meridian? Don't you think he's got the right to know?"

"Whose side are you on, anyhow?"

"I'm not on anybody's side. I'm just saying, I think he has the right to know, that's all."

"Well, I'm not keeping it. If that's what you're trying to do."

"I'm not trying to do anything. Jesus! I'm just saying you should tell him."

"Alright. I'll tell him then. But you're coming with me."

"What? Here? In a bar?"

"Yeah. Why not?"

When Meridian was done teasing her hair, we left and went back to our table. She told Chase she was pregnant, and he asked her how many guys she'd been sleeping with, and she told him two or three.

"Well, that's just perfect," he told her. "Two or three." Chase sucked the last few drops of Purple Haze from the mug and stood up, unfolding a wad of dollar bills and dropping the bills onto the table. "I think it's time we get you home, Hailey."

But we didn't go home, at least not right away, and of course, before we'd finally left, Meridian had somehow managed to convince Chase that she was sorry.

On the way home, all I could think about was Meridian and Chase having sex, his grimy hands crawling all over her body, his sloppy tongue worming its way into her ear. The angry part of me wanted to catch Chase with a butterfly knife while he was sleeping and pull a Lorena Bobbitt. I remembered the *Grey's Anatomy* episode I'd seen that talked about this tiny fish called the "penis fish" that lived in the Amazon River and swam into a man's penis while he was urinating into the water. The show said that after it swam up the man's penis, it ate through his insides. I imagined the fish chewing through the insides of Chase's pecker with its tiny little fish teeth. I even prayed to God that Meridian would come down with some awful venereal disease. As they kissed, I imagined little black eggs of herpes hatching in Meridian's ovaries, tiny little worms of syphilis wriggling through her salty veins.

After Chase dropped me off, I sat down on the steps outside listening to Mama and Daddy yelling inside. I sat there with my head between my knees, rocking back and forth, twisting one of the rubber snakes from my hair around my finger until the tip of my finger turned white. As I sat there, twisting the rubber snake around my finger, reciting the words to the Our Father over and over in my mind, I could feel the words beginning to burrow into my bones, each phrase like a song creeping down my backbone, from the tip of my brain, down to the tangled black roots of my feet. Before I knew it, I started to feel the way someone who's been hypnotized might feel, as if my thoughts were tiptoeing out of my skull. For almost an hour, I sat on those steps praying. Eventually, the yelling stopped, and I unfolded my hands and went inside.

*   *   *

The following morning, I heard a knock on the door. I looked out
the window and noticed a grey Chevy Avalanche. When I opened the
door, I couldn't believe who it was. It was Iris, and she was wearing
an orange flower dress, her hair pulled back in a ponytail. She wasn't
wearing the fake mole, but I couldn't help but imagine it, like a rotten
brown spot of melanoma growing on her cheek.

"Is Jules here?"

"No," I told her. I wanted to slap the lipstick off her ugly face.

"Okay then. Would you tell him I came by?" She turned around
and started walking back to her car.

"What do you want with my daddy?"

She turned around, and when she did, sunlight crawled across the
yard, catching her on the face. As she spoke, she held a cupped hand
across her forehead to shield her face from the sun. "I just wanted to
apologize for something I did. That's all."

"Are you the one who marked up his car?" I knew she'd done it,
but I wanted to see if she'd admit it.

She paused for a moment, still covering her face from the sun but
didn't say anything. She started to turn around again, but my words
stopped her.

"Don't you even care that your husband's dead?"

She paused, the sun bleeding across her face. "How do you know
about my husband?"

"I was there. In the car that night. Outside the strip club. I know
everything."

When I said this, her head bobbed toward the ground. She stared
at the ground for a moment, then glanced up at me. "You're just a
stupid kid. You don't know anything." She stared at me for a moment,
then turned around and walked to her truck. I slammed the door, and
went back inside. I could feel the anger climbing up my spine. I wanted
to stab my hand into her belly and rip out her black guts. I was so mad
that she'd come to my house. What if Mama would have been home?
She could have found out about the whole thing. As I was thinking this,

I ran into the kitchen, opened the refrigerator, grabbed two eggs and ran outside into the yard. As Iris was driving off, I hurled them toward her truck. One of them missed and landed in a patch of dead weeds. The other one hit the back window and splattered across the glass, dripping a yellow S of yoke downward.

Chapter Nineteen

The abortion clinic was on Gentilly Blvd., near an old run-down gas station. Earlier that morning, Meridian had called me to tell me that the pregnancy test she'd taken had come back positive. She said the clinic had an abortion pill that would get rid of the baby. She said the clinic had a strict policy. If you wanted to get an abortion, you had to be at least eighteen years old. And, you had to have proper ID to prove it. Convincing the clinic she was eighteen wasn't a problem for Meridian. She had the best damn fake ID I'd ever seen. It looked just like a Louisiana driver's license, and it said she was twenty-one. It worked at all the bars around town, and the clinic wasn't any different.

The waiting room inside the clinic had a balding secretary sitting behind a glass window. In the corner of the room was a table with a bouquet of plastic yellow flowers. There was a stack of magazines on the table, mostly with the usual bony airbrushed girls, each of them squeezed into some skimpy designer dress, smiling through their perfect white teeth.

After we waited a few minutes, a nurse came out and talked with Meridian. She said the doctor would begin by giving her an ultrasound to make sure Meridian was pregnant. After the ultrasound, the doctor would give her a pill that would kill the baby. Meridian had to take two more pills over the next two days. The nurse said Meridian would have to come back two weeks later for a follow-up appointment. After Meridian filled out some paperwork, a nurse took her back. While I sat in the waiting room, I thought about all the pictures I'd seen on the Internet, of baby heads crushed between forceps, little baby eyes and little baby hands stacked up in trash cans like piles of rotten meat.

I must have sat in the waiting room for almost two hours. On the way home I wanted to ask her how everything went, but I wasn't sure if she wanted to talk about it. Eventually, though, she brought it up.

"It's pretty crazy," she said. "how one little pill can change your whole life." She pulled a cigarette from her purse and lit it. "You know my momma had an abortion once."

"Really?"

Meridian took a long drag off the cigarette, flicked the ashes out the window. "Yeah. Before I was born."

"How old was she?"

"Sixteen, I think." Meridian glanced over at me, a smile drifting across her face. "I guess the rotten apple don't fall far from the tree, huh?"

"Did you tell her you were getting one?"

"Yeah."

"What did she say?"

"She was all for it. Told me I'd be better off letting my eggs rot than bringing some baby into the world." Meridian was picking at a chipped black fingernail. "My dad gave me his credit card and a box of condoms. Can you believe that? My family's so goddamn twisted."

"What about Chase? Did you two talk after you dropped me off last night?"

"Yeah. He said if I kept it, he'd help me take care of it. But I told him I wasn't keeping it. It's weird, after talking to him, I actually thought about keeping it."

"The baby?"

"Yeah. I think I woulda kept it, if it hadn't been mine, you know, if somebody woulda just left it on my doorstep or something. I dunno. Just the thought of some baby growing inside me. With the same eyes as me. The same lips. The same hair. It's enough to give me the creeps." Meridian flicked her cigarette into the grey air, then pulled down the sun visor and started teasing her hair. "It's probably for the best. I never did like babies anyhow. It's disgusting how helpless they are."

* * *

When I got home, I watched TV for a while. It was the last day of DON'T GO IN THE WATER WEEK on TNT, and *Jaws* was on again. Richard Dreyfuss was leaning over a wooden dock slicing a hole in the white belly of a tiger shark. I sat there, thinking about Chase, and the more I thought about him and Meridian and that baby, the more I started to feel like that shark, my guts ripped open, my insides spilling all over the floor.

By the time I got to school the next morning, herds of cars and pickups crawling with kids were pouring into the parking lot of Ben Franklin, clam shells crackling beneath their tires as their cars rattled past. Meridian was standing at the edge of the parking lot under a fig tree. As I walked up to her, she had on her usual pissed-off look, as if she wanted to scratch someone's eyes out.

"What's wrong?" I asked.

"You're a poisonous bitch," she said. "That's what's wrong." She took a drag off her cigarette, bit her lip, then blew the smoke out the corner of her mouth.

"What do you mean?"

"You know exactly what I mean, Hailey. Chase told me everything. Seems you two been having yourselves a little affair, huh?"

"Look, I'm sorry, alright. I didn't even think you liked him."

"You're so full of shit, Hailey. You knew damn well I liked him." She was so mad you could almost see the thoughts flying from her skull, like a swarm of angry blackbirds.

"Maybe he likes me, Meridian. Have you ever thought of that?"

"Come on, Hailey, do you really think Chase wants someone like you? Someone as average and dull as you?" Meridian laughed under her breath. "With your thrift store panties and your Calvin Clone jeans? Face it, guys are always gonna drool over me. That's just the way it is. I got the hips they like, the lips they like, the ass that wiggles the way they want it to."

"What are you talking about, Meridian? You're totally fake. Everything about you is fake. The way you act. The way you look."

"People like fake. Fake sells. You think some guys gonna want those sorry-ass tits of yours when they can have my perfect ones? What? Just 'cause they're real? The world's raised its standards, Hailey. Real just ain't good enough anymore."

"Let's go talk about this somewhere. We can skip Thibodeaux's class and come back for second period."

"You must be outta your skull, Girl. I'm not going anywhere with you. You and me are through."

"Meridian, please."

"I mean it, Hailey. You screwed with the wrong bitch this time." She took a drag off her cigarette, dropped it on the ground, and mashed it in the dirt with the toe of her red flat.

I watched her walk across the parking lot toward the front door of Ben Franklin. After she'd gone inside, I smoked a cigarette and then headed to first period.

Chapter Twenty

Two weeks had gone by since Mr. Guidry's death, and little cobwebs of grief had settled in my stomach. I couldn't stop thinking about the kid with the glass bones, his sad, cornflower blue eyes, his shiny black hair parted down the middle by a crooked line of white scalp, the blood clot like a tiny red flower blossoming his brain.

Chase hadn't returned any of my calls. I'd seen him once or twice picking up Meridian from school, but he acted different.

"Hey Hailey," he'd say, his candied yam arm wrapped around Meridian's neck, his eyes staring through me, the way Mama and Daddy stared through me, the way the whole world stared through me, like I was made of glass. I was beginning to feel like one of those lepers at the leper colony in Carville where Chase had wanted to take me on a date. Like some pitiful diseased girl who Jesus had forgotten to cure. I tried to get Chase's face out of my mind, but I couldn't. Even his name had become a black stone in my throat.

For months now, the roaches had been crawling around in my head, even worse than before. Sometimes I'd even hear voices ringing in my ears. At first, I thought that it was God speaking to me. But when I listened closely, the words started to sound like my own. I'd started to think more and more about swallowing a bottle of Mama's sleeping pills. When Mama worked at the hospital, she'd told me about all the attempted suicides she'd seen over the years, all the hangings gone wrong, the man whose throat looked like Swiss cheese after he drank a bottle of Drano, the woman who shattered all her bones, who had to wear a steel halo on her head after jumping off an overpass. Hanging yourself seemed so violent. With sleeping pills, I imagined a long, deep sleep. A tidy, clean death. No blood or bullets. Just a long, cloudy, pale white sleep.

The next morning, I waited for Daddy and Cyrus to leave the house. While Mama was asleep, I got a glass of water, then I went into her room and grabbed the bottle of sleeping pills from atop her dresser. When I got back to my room, I took the cap off the brown prescription bottle and poured the pills into my palm. They looked so holy in my hand, as if the bones of angels had been crushed into each perfect round pill. I swallowed a handful of the pills and chased it with a glass of water, then laid down on my bed, flat on my back.

For the first few minutes, nothing happened, so I closed my eyes and started to pray. "Our Father, who art in Heaven, hallowed be thy name." As I recited the prayer over and over, I could hear the words like the buzzing of yellow jackets in my ear. A wave of heat rolled over me, a stabbing pain blossomed in my toes and in the dark sockets of my eyes, then, a kind of short circuit in the wires of my brain, until the inside of my skull felt like a black sky exploding with stars.

*　　*　　*

The next thing I remember was waking up on a gurney at Touro. The room smelled like a mixture of rotten piss and baby powder. Daddy was asleep on a green cot next to my bed, his yellow bird's nest of hair dangling in his face. Mama was sitting on a chair at the foot of my bed, her hair pulled back in a ponytail, her cheeks smeared with mascara.

"How you feeling, Chickadee?" Daddy yawned, covering his mouth with a pale hand. He picked up a white styrofoam cup of coffee and blew on it.

"Okay, I guess."

Daddy stood up and stretched, exposing a mouthful of grey fillings as he arched his back. When he was done stretching, he sat down next to the bed and stroked my knuckles, his hand drifting just below the IV taped to the purple vein in my left hand. "Is your stomach feeling alright?"

"I'm sorry," I said, my voice cracking as I spoke.

"Yeah, well," Mama hissed. "It's a little late to be sorry, Hailey."

"Cut it out, Lena," Daddy snarled. "I mean it."

"I just hope you're happy, Hailey."

"Happy?" I asked. "Happy about what?"

Daddy stood up. "I mean it, Lena. Cut it out."

"What? That's what she wanted, Jules." Mama turned her eyes on me. "Wasn't that what you wanted, Hailey? For the whole world to finally know what a miserable family we are."

"No one's gonna find out anything, Lena. I dunno why you're so damned worried about what people think anyhow."

"My father didn't work his whole life building an empire to have us come along and ruin his family name."

"Empire? Jesus, Lena. He owned a goddamn department store for Christ's sake. Anyway, who cares what people think?"

"I care, Jules. I care."

The room grew quiet. Mama looked at Daddy then at me, then got up and walked out of the room.

"Don't worry about your momma," Daddy said, still stroking my knuckles. "She's just upset, that's all."

A few minutes later, a nurse came in and brought me dinner. It was the nastiest Hamburger Helper I'd ever seen, served with a side order of beets and an apple juice drink box. Cyrus had been gone for a while. I figured he'd probably finished smoking and gone looking for a doctor to look at the lump in his neck. Eventually, though, after I finished eating, he came back.

"Look what I got at the gift shop," he said, holding up a deck of cards. "You wanna play?"

Daddy yawned, scratching his pink head. "Sure. I'll play a few hands."

Cyrus grabbed the nightstand and put it between him and Daddy.

"Whatcha say?" he asked Daddy, shuffling the cards. "Poker? Aces Wild?"

Daddy grabbed his cup of coffee and took a sip. "Sounds good to me." He pressed his finger against the dry red scab in the corner of his mouth.

Cyrus glanced up at him, still shuffling the cards. "It still hurts?"

"Just when I open my mouth wide."

"Look. Daddy . . . about what I did."

"You don't need to apologize, Cyrus. I've spent most of my life giving you reasons to slug me."

Cyrus put his fan of cards face down on the table. "Yeah well, either way, it wasn't right of me to go and sock you like I did."

Daddy smiled, rearranging his cards. "Did I ever tell you about the time I socked your grandaddy?"

"Really? How old were you?"

Daddy licked his finger, still rearranging the cards in his hand. "'About nineteen I guess." Daddy slapped two cards down on the table. "Gimme two."

Cyrus dealt Daddy two cards, peeking at him from behind his poker hand. "Wasn't Grandaddy a boxer when he was young?"

"Yep. And he was meaner than dirt. You know that punching bag you're always hitting on? That was your grandaddy's."

"Really?" Cyrus pulled a pack of ginseng gum from his shirt pocket, bit off a piece, then crumbled the wrapper into his fist.

"Yep. He used to knock that thing around like it was stuffed with feathers."

"What did he do? When you hit him, I mean?"

"Nothing." Daddy licked his fingers, still rearranging the cards in his hand. "Didn't even flinch. Man had a goddamn iron jaw."

"Did he hit you back?"

"See this?" Daddy pointed a finger at a tiny scar above his yellow eyebrow.

Cyrus leaned in. "Yeah."

"Gave me that. And a pair of black eyes to go with it. In case you were wondering, you aren't the only son to ever hit their father."

Cyrus glanced up at Daddy and smiled. I watched them for a while, joking back and forth, swapping stories. When they were done, Cyrus left. Mama spent most of the afternoon praying. Daddy brought a copy of Shakespeare's sonnets from home, and he spent the evening sitting next to my bed reading to me.

*   *   *

Later that night, I woke to the crackle of thunder, imagining the black rain falling outside my window. All the lights were off, and in the corner of the room, I could see the bright orange tip of a cigarette glowing in the dark. Above the cigarette, two white eyes floated in the black air. "Cyrus?" I called out. "That you?"

"It's me, Miss Hailey," the voice said.

The lights flicked on. It was Moses.

"I didn't scare you, did I?" he asked.

"No. I thought you were Cyrus. What time is it?"

Moses turned his wrist over and tapped the face of the watch. "Bout eleven, I spose." He took a drag off his Kool, blew the smoke out his nose, stood up, and walked over to the sink, turned the water on and put the cigarette under the trickle of water. "How you holding up?"

"All right I guess." I watched the white smoke from Moses's cigarette hover in the air like a ghost. "Just bored."

"I'll bet. Anything I can do?"

"Actually, I have an itch on my nose. Can you undo the strap on my wrist so I can scratch it?"

Moses paused for a moment. "Tell you what . . . how about if I scratch it for you. How's that?"

He walked over to the side of my bed. "Where's it at?" he asked, staring down at my stomach while he spoke, his mildewed breath drifting in the air.

He rested a dirt-caked fingernail on my stomach. His finger wormed its way toward my silver belly ring, his shriveled black hand creeping over my skin like a tarantula. "Didn't know you had a belly ring." He grinned, his gold tooth flickering as he spoke. His finger crept toward my nose and scratched the tip, his eyes still drifting over my stomach. "How's that? Better?"

"Thanks."

He sat back down in the chair. "So," he asked me, "who all's been by to see you?" As he spoke, he stared at me, his eyes tracing the blue veins in my neck.

"Just my mom and dad. And Cyrus." I smiled. "And now you."

"Cyrus, huh?" he said, smiling with the same yellow teeth. "Cyrus came by here?"

"Yep."

"Did he say where he was going?"

"Home, I guess."

Moses paused for a moment. "Cops ain't been by to see you, Miss Hailey, have they?" He stared around the room as he spoke, his words floating in the air, his voice like a hand on my shoulder.

"Nope."

"That's good." He rubbed his cheek with an ashy brown hand. "That's real good," he mumbled, with a faraway look, as if he was talking to himself, the words sprouting like weeds in his head. He sat back in his chair, his pot belly poking out of his shirt as he bit at a toothpick between his lips. "Look, Miss Hailey, this ain't exactly a personal visit." He moved the toothpick around in his mouth while he spoke. "I got a few questions need answering, and I'm hoping you can help me with a few answers." He took the toothpick out of his mouth, picking at a piece of food between his teeth.

"What kind of questions?"

"Well." He wiped the toothpick on the tail of his shirt and began picking his teeth again, staring at me through the worm holes of his eyes. "Seems that brother of yours has been squealing to the cops."

"Cyrus? Are you sure?"

"Oh, I'm sure. My friend Smiley works over at the police station. Apparently, Cyrus told the cops a batch of lies about me. Claiming I was the one killed that baby molester in Algiers." His voice changed, and I could almost smell the stink of rotting bodies buried in his words. "I don't know what kinda silly thoughts that brother of yours has got cooking in that skull of his," he said, "but he needs to keep that snatch of his shut. You tell him, if anybody mentions my name, anybody, there's gonna be Hell to pay. I'll root 'em out personally, Miss Hailey, and I won't stop till I squeeze every ounce of Jesus from their rotten little souls."

I wanted to tell him to leave Cyrus alone, that if he hurt my brother, I'd go straight to the cops. I wanted to scare him the way he was scaring me. But I didn't say a word. Instead, I just sat there, the words melting like a peppermint in my mouth.

Just then, a nurse in a white uniform walked into the room.

"Visiting hours are over, Sir," she told Moses, her eyes ice, a metal clipboard clutched against her chest.

Moses got up from the chair. "Guess they kicking me out, Miss Hailey."

The nurse walked to the side of the bed. While she fiddled with my IV, Moses put a finger to his lips, and whispered SHHHHHHHHH. The nurse leaned over me and Moses disappeared behind her. After she had changed the IV, I looked up, and Moses was gone.

Chapter Twenty-one

When I woke up the next morning, a silver cloud of pigeons was flapping outside the window. I spent the morning watching TV. Mama and Daddy came by around eleven. A few minutes after they got there, a man in a white coat came in. He introduced himself and walked over to the side of my bed. He was a tall man with pink Pepto-Bismol colored lips and a brown toupee the color of a dog turd.

"I'm Doctor Gaudet," he said. "I came by to see how you're doing, Hailey. Are you feeling alright today?"

"I'm okay, I guess."

"Any suicidal thoughts, depression?"

"Not really."

"Are the medications keeping you relaxed?"

"Yeah, I guess. I've been sleeping a lot."

"That's perfectly normal. The medications we're giving you are designed to make you relax."

The doctor turned to Mama and Daddy, adjusting his brown turd toupee as he spoke. "Have you spoken with the nurse about a psychiatric facility?"

"Yes." Mama told him. "We'll be sending her to River Oaks."

"Actually," Daddy interrupted, "we can't afford River Oaks, but Charity can take her."

"This is no time to pinch pennies, Jules." Mama forced a smile. "Our daughter just tried to kill herself for God's sake."

"They're both wonderful facilities," the doctor said, smiling with his pink Pepto-Bismol lips. "The nurse'll be by in a few minutes with the necessary paperwork. I'd like to get Hailey in today, if possible."

When he was finished, the doctor shook Daddy's hand and left.

A few minutes later, a nurse came in with a packet of papers.

"Okay," she told Mama and Daddy, "I have the paperwork for you to sign. Since Hailey's a minor, we'll need one of you to sign."

The nurse handed the papers to Daddy. He put his glasses on the tip of his nose and started reading the paper, following each line of writing with the tip of his pen. While Daddy read the papers, the nurse handed Mama a pink brochure. "Here's some information concerning various psychiatric disorders. Shortly after Hailey arrives, a psychiatrist will be assigned to her. Once he provides a diagnosis, you'll have a better idea of what you're dealing with."

Daddy scribbled his signature at the bottom of the paper in dark black ink. "How long does she stay there?" Daddy asked, handing the paper back to the nurse.

"It's difficult to say, really. The state requires a minimum of three days after a suicide attempt. But often the psychiatrist will recommend additional treatment. She'll be in good hands, Mr. and Mrs. Trosclair. I assure you."

*　　*　　*

Charity was in downtown New Orleans. I got there around ten o'clock that night and kissed Mama and Daddy goodbye before a big black man named Clarence introduced himself. He had shiny, black patent leather skin, and his eyes looked like blackberries floating in a pool of milk. He walked me over to a separate building, locking each door behind him with a large silver ring of keys. Once inside, he took my blood pressure and asked if I was wearing a belt. After I told him no, he asked me to pull my shoe strings out of my shoes and balled them into his big black fist. I found out later that a kid had hanged himself with the orange shoestrings from his Nike high-tops. Little did I know then, but this would become the only way of figuring out who was who during Visiting Hours. The visitors had shoestrings. The patients didn't.

When Clarence was done, he gave me a pill and a cup of water and showed me to my room. I asked him what the pill was called and he said it was Seroquel. When I got to my room, I noticed that the bed next to mine looked as if someone had been sleeping in it. On the nightstand next to the bed was a bouquet of yellow tulips with a note that read: WE MISS YOU CHLOE. I put my clothes on, climbed into bed, and fell asleep.

*   *   *

The next morning I woke to the sound of a man's voice. It was Clarence. "Hailey . . . Chloe, time for group." I looked across the room and saw a woman in a pink robe with a rat's nest of blonde hair. She looked at me for a minute then left the room. After I got dressed, Clarence led me down a hallway to a room with a large wooden door. As I entered the room, I noticed a group of people sitting in a circle. I found a chair and sat down. A lady with starched white slacks and a pink rayon blouse closed the door behind me and introduced herself. Her name was Penny, and she spoke with a slow Mississippi drawl. Her long blonde hair was tucked behind her ears. A diamond ring flickered on her finger.

"How is everyone today?" Penny asked. "Why don't we start with you, Raynelle?"

Penny was staring at a large black woman who had dark black holes for eyes and a brain of braids pinned to her skull. The black woman didn't answer, only stared back at Penny blankly, as if she was turning the words over in her mind.

"Are you doing alright today, Raynelle?" Penny asked. "How are the voices? Are the voices back?"

Raynelle stared at her for a moment. "They talking again."

"So the medicine's not working?" Penny fiddled with the gold necklace dangling around her neck as she spoke.

"I just said they talking again," Raynelle told her. "Ain't the medicine sposed to stop the voices from talking?"

"It's supposed to," Penny grinned, her smile like a jack-o-lantern's smile, as if someone had carved it into her face.

"All right then." Raynelle stared at Penny as if she was waiting for Penny to say something, as if she wanted to ram her hand down Penny's throat and yank the words out.

"My medicine's working," Chloe smiled, scratching a leg streaked with a purple spider web of varicose veins. "My medicine's working just fine."

"That's wonderful, Chloe," Penny said, smiling with the same jack-o-lantern smile.

Chloe took a sip of coffee and cleared her throat. She straightened her pink robe and ran her hand through her rat's nest of blond hair, exposing a clump of black roots. "I see angels wherever I go," she said, picking at a pimple on her neck. She paused for a moment, her voice flopping like a stunned fish, as if a thought was stuck in the tiny silver gears of her brain. "Dirty little angels. With dirty little mouths. And dirty little hands."

Raynelle grinned, lipstick on her teeth. "What they dirty for?"

"What?" Chloe asked, turning her eyes on Raynelle.

"The angels," Raynelle asked. "You said their hands and mouth is dirty. What they dirty for?"

Chloe looked at Raynelle as if the answer were obvious. "They have to eat our souls before we can go to Heaven," she told her. "The dirt's from our souls. It rubs off on their hands and their mouths when they eat it."

"Lord have mercy." Raynelle scratched an itch deep in the black brain of her braids, a laugh gurgling in her throat. "And you think your medicine's working. Hell, you as looney as you ever was."

"What about you, Maynard?" Penny asked. "How are you feeling today?"

Penny was staring at a skinny man with leathery skin. He had two bright blue eyes, a grey goatee, and a tan line the shape of a watch on his wrist. "Me?" Maynard asked, scratching his grey goatee with his dry, calloused fingers. "I'm just waiting for my sister to call. Did she call yet? She said she was gonna call."

"Not yet," Penny answered. "I called her, though."

"How are you feeling?" Penny asked again.

"How am I feeling?" Maynard repeated. "I'd be fine if it weren't for Clarence."

"As some of you may already know," Penny said, smiling with the same Jack-O-lantern smile, "Clarence and Maynard had an incident last night."

"A incident?" Maynard smirked. "Is that what you call it? A incident?" Maynard glanced over at me, blowing on his coffee. He took a sip and smiled, exposing two missing teeth. "Some big Democrat pumped up on steroids straps you down to your bed and they call it a incident."

While I smiled back at Maynard, a man barked at Penny from across the room.

"Where the Frosted Flakes went, Miss Penny?" He was a tall thin black man with gold teeth, and he had a tattoo of a scorpion on the back of his hand. "Been waiting for Frosted Flakes for two days now. Whatcha gotta do to get a damn bowl of Frosted Flakes around here?"

"They should be in the kitchen drawer." Penny told him, fixing the collar of her pink rayon blouse. "Below the microwave."

"Should be," the man told her, "but they ain't. I'd kill for a goddamned bowl of Frosted Flakes."

"Hailey," Penny said, fiddling with her gold necklace again. "Would you like to tell us what brought you here?"

I stared back at her for a moment and shook my head.

"That's fine." Penny responded. "You can talk when you're ready."

After group was over, I tried calling Cyrus at home. I was lucky. He'd just gotten home. I told him Moses had stopped by to see me the night before, and that he thought Cyrus had gone to the cops and ratted him out, but Cyrus said he hadn't said a word. I told him he'd better sprout eyes in the back of his head until things blew over. He didn't seem too worried, though. He asked me how I was doing, and I told him I'd been transferred to Charity Psych Ward. He said he'd be sure to come and visit me with Mama and Daddy.

I spent the rest of the day in my room reading a book I'd found. I tried to keep to myself. To be honest, most of the people scared me to death. Clarence had told me that in the past patients had been separated by age and diagnosis, but that a lack of funding had forced them to put everyone in the same wing of the ward. The place was filled with Meth heads and schizophrenics, alcoholics, bulimics, crack addicts. You name it, they were there. Most of them wandered around the ward mumbling to themselves. Others curled up in blankets on the couch chain-smoking cigarettes.

During my first day, I'd spoken to a few of them. One of the Meth addicts, a black-haired girl with ponytails and pink acne. She reminded me of Mary-Ann from *Gilligan's Island*. She'd come up to me a few times, scratching her face as she spoke, asking me if I saw any bugs on her face. When I told her no, she turned around and asked me to check and see if I saw any bugs crawling through her dirty black hair.

Later that afternoon, a large black man with two missing teeth came over and told me that the FBI was in the walls of the Psych Ward. He said they were talking to him from the wires in the walls. Clarence said that the man had been in the military and that the night before, he'd punched a hole the size of a fist in one of the sheetrock walls of his room, trying to pull the wires out the walls. The man spent most of his time in front of the TV. Every few minutes, he'd stand up in his furry brown Yosemite Sam slippers and salute the air.

*   *   *

At dinner, I sat by myself, watching Chloe twist a leg off a deep-fried turkey, scooping a spoonful of corn onto her plate. She grabbed a Coke from the kitchen and sat down next to me. I said hello, but she didn't say a word. I watched her smash the kernels of corn with the tines of her fork.

"They plant microphones in here, you know?" she told me.

"Microphones?" I asked.

"Yep," Chloe said. "They plant 'em in other things too, but mostly the corn." She looked at me for a moment and smiled. I paused for a second, and smiled back at her, grinning as I smashed each yellow kernel of corn with the tines of my fork.

Chapter Twenty-two

By the second day, my brain was buzzing like a hornet's nest, and I could feel my blood like a swarm of electric currents crackling through my veins. That morning, I told my psychiatrist, and he said the medication would take a few days to work. I was getting worried about Cyrus. I was scared that Moses had hurt him. I tried calling home, but no one answered.

Later that day, I noticed that a new patient had been admitted. She was a black woman from the 9th Ward named Lavonia. Her hair was a clump of colored beads, her mouth the pink petals of an azalea. She said she owned a voodoo store in the French Quarter and that the police had locked her up in Charity for casting spells on people.

That afternoon, Mama and Daddy came to visit me during visiting hours. When they arrived, I asked them where Cyrus was, and they said that he'd been staying with my cousin Moonie for a few days. I was relieved to hear that Cyrus wasn't in New Orleans, especially after what Moses had said a few days ago.

We sat on an orange vinyl sofa by the window. Mama kissed me on the cheek and sat down. "So," Mama said, "you doing all right? Nobody in here's tried to molest you yet, have they?"

"What the Hell kind of thing is that to ask?" Daddy snarled, his face nicked up from shaving, freckled with tiny pieces of bloody toilet paper.

"I saw this special on *60 Minutes* that said girls in these places are always getting molested." Mama peeled back a yellow label marked VISITOR and pressed it against her breast. "I'm just making sure my daughter's safe, that's all."

Daddy sat down and hugged me, a white styrofoam cup of coffee steaming in his hand. "I don't want you to worry about anything, Chickadee. This is a top notch facility. Miss Verma says Charity is the Holiday Inn of Mental Hospitals."

Mama reached into her purse, glancing over at me as she spoke. "Smells more like the Motel 6 if you ask me." She pulled a tiny bottle of Instant Hand Sanitizer from her purse, and squirted a small lump into her palm. "For the record, I wanted to put you in River Oaks, but of course your father said we couldn't afford it. You know I heard they actually have room service, even cable TV. All the famous politicians and celebrities in New Orleans stay there."

"Jesus, Lena, it's not a goddamn resort. It's a hospital for Christ's sake."

"I'm just saying, you might as well stay in the best place possible."

"I'm sorry, Hailey," Daddy said. "We just couldn't afford it."

"You don't have to apologize, Daddy."

"Where are your shoestrings?" Mama asked.

I pulled at the white tongue of my shoe, wiping at a grey scuff mark the shape of a crescent moon on the toe of my white tennis shoe. "They took them."

"Why'd they take your shoestrings?"

"It's a security measure," Daddy said, blowing on his coffee. "So they don't go and hang themselves with 'em."

"Well that's just ridiculous. No child of mine is gonna hang themselves with a set of shoestrings. How are you supposed to get around when your feet are falling outta your shoes?"

"They give you twist ties," I said, still wiping at the grey scuff mark on the toe of my shoe. "I just forgot to go and get them."

Mama crossed her legs and glanced down at the yellow sticker on her blouse. She pulled the yellow sticker off her blouse, repositioned it, and pressed it against her breast again. She looked up at the ceiling for a minute, then glanced over at me. "Look Hailey. I'm sorry, all right? I guess this whole thing's my fault. Maybe if I'd been a better mother, none of this woulda happened. A good mother doesn't sit up in the bed and rot all day, ignoring her children."

As Mama said this I thought about what Verma had said, about how it wasn't right for me to blame somebody for the life I was dealt, about how I was the only one who could make sure my life turned out the way I wanted it. "It's not your fault. I've been spending so much time trying to figure out who I should blame. It's not your fault this happened."

Daddy sat down next to Mama and rested his hand on her shoulder. "I prayed last night, Hailey. I did. I told Jesus if he protected my baby from all the nut jobs in this hospital, I wouldn't drink a drop of liquor ever again. I emptied the refrigerator of all the beer. Even poured all the wine down the sink. There's not a drop of liquor left in the house. And when I get home, I'm gonna take that pint of Vodka I got in the glovebox in my Nova and throw it in the trash."

Mama wiped her eyes with the sleeve of her shirt, mascara smeared across her face. "He did. He threw it all out. Verma came over and had a long talk with us both. She says she can get him a job down at Wal-Mart."

Mama and Daddy smiled and we hugged each other for a while. When they were leaving, I told Daddy I was lonely, and that the only pets Charity allowed were fish. He said he'd bring me a goldfish when he came by the following day.

After Mama and Daddy left, Lavonia taught Chloe how to cast a spell on someone. I watched them sit together all night, smiling, Chloe staring in amazement at Lavonia as she drew X's in the air, mumbling spells under her breath. I spent the rest of the night watching TV. There was a documentary on FOX called *Cosmetic Surgeries Gone Wrong*, and there was this scrawny lady with fat collagen lips and peroxide-streaked hair, and she was talking about her botched lipo suction surgery. The skin on her stomach was scarred from the surgery and it looked like a lump of chewed meatloaf. When she was finished blabbering about her lip surgery, they interviewed another woman whose right nipple turned black and rotted off after she got a botched boob job. As I watched the documentary, I couldn't help but think about Meridian. I smiled, imagining her collagen lips swelling up, like the pair of wax lips I used to wear at Halloween, the little rubber sacks in her boobs rupturing in her chest, her rotten nipples crying little crystal tears of silicone.

*   *   *

The next morning I woke to the sound of orderlies pushing a gurney down the hall. Lavonia was in the kitchen eating a bowl of cereal. I asked her what had happened, and she said that Raynelle had killed herself. Apparently, after being put on suicide watch, Raynelle had cracked the light bulb dangling from the ceiling and used it to slit her throat.

That day in group, everyone talked about how much they missed Raynelle. Chloe spent most of the day crying, walking around in her ragged, yellow robe, running her fingers through her rat's nest of blonde hair, mascara smeared across her cheek.

Chloe and Raynelle had been friends for years. Clarence said they'd spent most of their lives in and out of psychiatric hospitals, and that they'd crossed paths over the years. For most of the day, Lavonia and I played checkers and smoked cigarettes. Lavonia said she was working on a batch of spells that would help Chloe get through her grief.

That afternoon, when Mama and Daddy came to visit me, they brought me a bright orange goldfish. After they left, I spent most of the evening watching the fish swim around in circles, feeling just like it must have felt, as if a pane of glass somehow separated me from the rest of the world, as if I'd spent my whole life, like that fish, gasping for air, slowly drowning.

Around ten o'clock, after I got my meds, I noticed Chloe in our room by the sink, crushing a white pill in the basin. I asked her why she was putting her medicine down the sink, and she told me that she didn't like the medicine. She said she never swallowed the pills the hospital gave her. That the pills chased the angels away. She said she'd found a way to hide the pills in her cheek so that the nurses thought she'd swallowed them.

That night, for some reason, I dreamed that all my teeth had fallen out. Nobody had punched them out. They'd simply fallen out, by themselves. Just before the dream ended, I was standing in the front of a mirror, grinning with a toothless smile, my tongue sucking on the bloody holes where the teeth had been.

Chapter Twenty-three

The following day, Chloe and Lavonia and I went to art therapy. The instructor was a fat lady with a thin black moustache and a ponytail of black hair. She gave us crayons, markers, and paper, and told us to draw whatever we wanted. Chloe drew a picture of a skinny girl with long strands of orange hair standing under a maroon sky. She said it was her daughter. The girl's hair looked like flames burning atop her head. Lavonia drew a self portrait. A big black face with lips the shape of a red hookworm and silver stars for eyes. I drew a picture of me, Mama, Daddy, and Cyrus holding hands under a yellow sky filled with black clouds.

After Art Therapy, we watched TV for a while. That night, Mama and Daddy couldn't make visiting hours, so, I went to my room to read for a while. After I got my meds, I spent the rest of the night watching Lavonia and Chloe play checkers.

When I woke the following day, I checked the *Times Picayune*. The day before, they'd interviewed the parents of the kid with the glass bones, saying that a bunch of kids had been questioned. Today, there was nothing except a small picture of the kid with the glass bones in the right corner of the front page. Underneath the picture, there was a line that read: REWARD $1000 FOR INFORMATION LEADING TO THE ARREST AND CONVICTION OF SUSPECT(S) IN CORY RABALAIS CASE. I was worried that Cyrus was in jail. Or even worse, that Moses had gotten his hands on him.

I spent two more days at Charity. They released me on Saturday, and Daddy came to pick me up. On the way home, Daddy stopped at the supermarket to get a loaf of bread. As we pulled into the parking lot, I spotted Iris's grey Chevy Avalanche. Just as Daddy killed the car, Iris came out with a pack of cigarettes clenched in her teeth, a six pack of Colt 45 under each arm. She winked at us and climbed into her truck, cranked the engine, and shoved it into drive. As she peeled out the parking lot, she stuck her skinny white arm out the window and flipped us off.

When we got to the house, the sky was empty except for a line of crows stretched across the horizon like a huge black headline. Cyrus's Hyundai was parked in the yard, but I didn't see him outside or in the house. I'd brought the goldfish home from the hospital, but it didn't make it home alive. It was floating near the top of the water, a white film covering its eyes. I could see the tiny red veins in his white belly. I said a prayer and flushed it down the toilet. After I finished unpacking, I went into the kitchen. Mama said that a few people had left messages for me while I was in the hospital. They were mostly from relatives, one from my grandma and one from Verma. I was surprised to see that one of them was from Meridian. Mama said she'd actually come by twice while I was in Charity. As I was listening to the message, I heard a knock at the door. It was Meridian.

"Hey Kid," she winked. She was wearing a white half shirt. She had her hair in pig-tails, and she was holding a bouquet of fresh sunflowers. "Heard you were in the hospital." She handed me the bouquet of sunflowers. "These are for you."

I smiled. "I thought you were mad at me?"

She grinned with her fat collagen lips. "Christ, Hailey. Can't a person do one nice thing in their life?"

I smiled. "I didn't know you had a heart."

"I have one," she said. "It's just black. That's all."

I laughed.

"So, you doing alright?" Meridian asked.

"Yeah. I'm good I guess."

"Hey, since it's your first day back, I thought you might like to go to a party. You up for it?"

"Yeah. Sure. Sounds fun. Where at?"

"We're planning on getting a keg and camping out at an old abandoned house on Leonidas Street." She pulled an orange card out of her pocket. "Here's some directions. This should get you there."

"Thanks, Meridian. I really appreciate it."

"You can even bring Cyrus if you want to."

"Yeah, he'll probably give me a ride. I think he's got the hots for you."

Meridian smiled. "What can I say?" She batted her eyelashes, and they looked like spiders crawling out of her eyes. "Gotta give the boys what they want."

When we were done talking, I walked Meridian outside to her car. Cyrus was on the porch, shirtless, the silver muscles in his arms flickering in the sun, a red punching bag dangling from a hook in the porch ceiling where a wooden swing had been. He was such a show-off. As Meridian pulled off, Cyrus waved to her, a goofy grin on his lips.

"Hey Sis," he said, wrapping his wrist with a roll of white tape, tearing a piece off with his teeth. "I didn't know you were home. You feeling better?"

I grabbed a black boxing glove from the ground and held it for him while he rammed his fist deep into the glove. "Yeah." I grabbed the other red glove from the ground and held it for him, as I'd done with the first. "You know Meridian just invited me to a party tonight."

"Come on. Don't joke with me like that." He hit the gloves together, then grabbed the black bag to steady it against the air.

"She did. And she invited you too."

He caught the bag as it swung from the side to side, holding it steady against the air. "Where's it at?"

"On Leonidas Street."

"Good." He hit the bag again, this time with a right jab and then a left hook. "I'm starting to get creeped out around here anyway."

"Yeah. Mama said you been staying at Moonie's in Covington."

He steadied the bag for a moment. "Yep. I just came back today to see you. I'm thinking of going back there tonight, probably after that party. I'm still a little worried that Moses might come looking for me." Cyrus paused for a moment. "Looks like the whole thing was a set up."

"What do you mean?"

"I talked to Brian Berton, that kid who works over at Blockbuster. He said Moses's daughter lives in Algiers, and that a while back, she was supposedly molested by some young kid over there."

"Jesus. That's right. He told me his daughter lives in Algiers."

"Guess he wanted revenge or something, who knows. I've been trying to lay low." Cyrus socked the bag, first with a left jab, then with a right hook. He steadied the bag again, wiping silver beads of sweat from his forehead with the back of the black boxing glove. "What was it like in there, anyway? Charity I mean?"

I pulled a cherry Now and Later from my pocket and unwrapped it. "It wasn't that bad." I balled the plastic wrapper into my fist and stuck it in my pocket. "Seemed like everybody was as screwed up as me. Some of them even worse off than I was."

Cyrus socked the bag with a right jab, then a left. "The world's a pretty screwed up place, Little Sis." He held the bag steady for a moment, and socked it again, biting his lip as he hit it with a right hook. "Daddy said they gave you some medicine. Is it helping any?"

"Yeah. I'm starting to feel better."

"That's good."

I told him I was going to see Verma. He said to be back home before seven so we could go to the party.

"It's nice to have you back," he said, turning toward the bag again and then socking it with a left jab.

As I walked down the clam-shell driveway, I saw him glance over his shoulder, waving at me with the large black boxing glove as I headed toward the blacktop.

* * *

When I got to Verma's, she was sitting in her usual lawn chair in the courtyard of her apartment complex, near the edge of the pool, wearing her pink robe, a bowl of grapes in her lap. "What's wrong?" she asked, as I walked up. "Ain't you ever seen a woman with one leg before?"

I told her all about Charity. How sometimes my thoughts crawled around like roaches in my head. She said years back she had checked herself into a psychiatric hospital after her husband had hanged himself.

"I wrastled with depression for years," she said, reaching into the bowl in her lap for another grape. "After Malcolm killed himself, I felt like I was losing my wits. My brain was all scrambled." Verma put the grape in her mouth. "Felt like my thoughts was all lumped together like oatmeal. Some days, I couldn't even get up out the bed." She peeled the skin off the grape and stuck it in her mouth, sucking on it as she spoke. "That depression. It hits you like a Mac truck."

"How'd you get past it?" I reached into Verma's lap and grabbed a grape.

"It just went away eventually. Important thing is to see a therapist once a week after you get out. It's kinda like a booster shot, you know. To get through the week."

"Yeah." I sucked on the grape while I spoke. "They said I needed to see a social worker, but Mama said they're expensive."

"Well, don't you worry about that. Me and your momma worked all that out."

"What do you mean?"

Verma spit a seed over her shoulder. "I'm gonna help your momma pay for it."

"I don't want you to do that, Verma."

"Well, it ain't up to you. How 'bout that?"

Verma spit another seed over her shoulder then adjusted her beige mannequin leg, sucking on a grape in her cheek as she spoke. "It's my money, and I'll do what I want with it." She scratched her good leg with her fingernail, her stockings rolled to her ankles like a tourniquet. I asked her how she was doing. She said she still had pain in her ghost foot, and that sometimes she woke up thinking she had her leg.

"It don't make no sense. It's like my brain ain't told my leg it's gone. I liked to fell down getting outta bed the other night. Thinking I still had my leg."

"Are you getting around okay? With the new leg, I mean?"

"Sure. Still feels kinda strange, you know, plugging some plastic leg into my hip every day. But Hell, I'm grateful. Least I got one good leg left. My grandmomma lost *both* her legs fore she died."

"Really? I didn't know that."

"Yep. She was in a wheel chair till the day she died."

"Did your momma have diabetes too?"

"Yep. Runs in my family. On my momma's side."

"When I was in the hospital, they asked me if depression ran in my family. Turns out, I may have gotten it from Mama."

"Yep. It all gets passed down. Just like everything else." Verma chewed on the grape as she spoke. "It's terrible, sometimes," she said, spitting a seed over her shoulder. "The things parents pass down to they kids."

"Yeah, it's kind of depressing actually."

"Just take your medicine and go to your therapy sessions like they told you, and you'll be fine. You probably just got too much time on your hands. Maybe when I get your daddy that job down at Wal-Mart, we'll get you one too. You could use a little responsibility. Your momma shoulda made you get a job a long time ago, anyhow. Hell, I had a full-time job by the time I was thirteen."

Verma told me about the job she had when she was thirteen, how she worked in a candy factory with her cousin Catina for almost two years. We talked for a while. Before I left, Verma handed me an envelope to give to Mama. It wasn't sealed, so on the way home, I opened it. There was money inside and a note that said: DEAR LENA, HERE'S SOME MONEY TO GET OUR LITTLE GIRL'S LIFE RIGHT, LOVE VERMA.

Chapter Twenty-four

The abandoned house where the party was being held was nothing more than an old, rotten, shotgun-double surrounded by weeds. Meridian's Buick was there, along with a few other cars. As we got out the car, Meridian poked her head out and yelled to us from a smaller building next to the house. I told Cyrus I was starting to get a bad feeling about the whole thing, but he was too concerned with the possibility of screwing Meridian to care. We followed her voice, past a stack of old tires, corroded pipes, piles of lumber and rolls of chain-link fence, until we came to what looked like an old rotten tool shed with a tar-paper roof. As we walked up, Meridian was standing in the doorway.

It was a big room with rotted mildewed boards for walls, and the floor was covered with sawdust. There was a drill press and a table saw in the middle of the room, a hammer hung on the wall with two rusty nails. The windows were cracked, the window sills freckled with dead flies. The only light in the room came from a single light bulb dangling from a long wire pinned to the ceiling by a nail. As we walked in, I noticed a few guys I didn't know in the room. One of the boys nodded to me. He was a big muscular black kid with a shiny black head, his teeth clenching a dead cigar. The other boy was a muscular white kid with pale, pocked skin, long, nappy blonde dread locks, and gold teeth. I was looking at the white kid, when I felt something behind me. Before I knew what had happened, somebody pulled my arms behind my back, and put a knife to my throat. At the same time, the black kid put Cyrus in a full nelson. "Meridian, you bitch," Cyrus growled, choking on the words, his eyes rolled toward the dusty ceiling, a blue spider web of veins bulging in his neck.

"Shut your damn mouth," the white kid yelled, pressing the knife against my throat. "Else I'll gut her like a fish." I could feel his dirty breath on my neck, the blade of the knife sharp and cold against my throat.

A knot of muscles rippled in the black kid's arms, his mouth clenched so tight he looked lipless. He pushed Cyrus to the ground and started kicking him in the ribs. Cyrus was on his hands and knees, spitting blood onto the splintered floor.

Meridian was leaning against the drill press, smirking at me from across the room. Every molecule in me wanted to smash that pretty face of hers. Somehow I managed to squirm from the boy's grip. I leaped across the room and smacked Meridian in her face. As she tried to balance herself against the wall, I grabbed a fistful of her hair and dragged her to the ground. The white kid pulled me off Meridian, and wrapped his thick muscled arms around me so that I couldn't move.

Meridian stumbled to her feet, her hair hanging in her face. She pushed her hair from her eyes, wiping bits of sawdust from her hair. As I watched Cyrus, I noticed someone in the corner of my eye, walking into the room. It was Moses. "Good," he said, scratching an itch through a ragged arm hole in his robe, his gold tooth shining in the dirty light. "We're all here. You can go, Miss Meridian."

Meridian walked over to Moses and kissed him on the cheek. When she got to the door, she winked at me and left. Moses walked over to Cyrus, slowly, casually.

"Well," he said. "If it ain't the Mouth of the South, Cyrus Trosclair." He nudged Cyrus, first in the rib with the tip of his shoe, then kicking him square in the gut. "Can't seem to keep that rat hole of yours shut. Can ya?" He looked around the room for a moment, then bent down toward Cyrus, the dark rust of his voice growing soft. "You a endangered species, Boy, and you don't even know it. I got mind to make you eat a bullet for what you did."

The roaches were crawling in my head again. I could feel my heart like a purple fist beating against the bony cage of my ribs. I wanted to crawl out of my skin, leap across the room and scratch Moses'ss face off, crack his skull open with the hammer hanging on the wall and snatch the light from his eyes. But the knife was pressed hard against my throat.

While I watched Moses, I noticed the bald black kid bending toward the ground. He plugged one of the extension cords into an old junction box and lifted Cyrus's limp arm onto the table. The boy turned a switch near the saw, and the ragged teeth of the blade began to hum. He held Cyrus's hand flat against the table, prying Cyrus's index finger from his clenched fist. Cyrus's skin was white as a maggot, and his eyes were bulging in their sockets.

As the black kid moved Cyrus's finger toward the blade, Moses began to speak loudly, his voice rising over the hum of the saw, gnawing at the air. "Let the lying lips be put to silence. He that worketh deceit shall not dwell within my house."

I closed my eyes and Cyrus began to scream. I listened to his black screams grow louder and louder until they slowly drowned beneath Moses's voice. I wanted to scream too, but the words crawled to the back of my throat.

"He that telleth lies shall not tarry in my sight," Moses said. "For the mouth of the wicked and the mouth of the deceitful are opened against me: they have spoken against me with a lying tongue."

I kept my eyes closed for what seemed like forever. I could hear Moses's voice buzzing in my ears. The thoughts were loose in my head, and I was beginning to feel like I was leaving my body. When I started to feel my thoughts drifting away from me, I opened my eyes and noticed Cyrus balled up on the floor, his face and hair caked with sawdust and blood. Then, the bald black kid cut the switch on the saw, and for a moment, the air grew still. Moses stared down at Cyrus, his face cold and hard. "Tomorrow, you gonna go down and see the police. You tell 'em you was the one that killed that baby molester, or I'm gonna come looking for you again. And next time I ain't gonna be so nice." He kicked at Cyrus. "You understand?"

Moses turned toward me and pulled the blue comb from his afro, combing the tiny black hairs of his moustache. "Turn her loose."

When he said this, the white kid with the dreadlocks let me go. I bolted across the room to where Cyrus was, first helping him to his feet, then walking him toward the door. Once I'd gotten him out of the shed, I walked him past the pile of rotten tires and rolls of chainlink fence, until we came to his Hyundai. I put him in the car and climbed into the driver's seat, grabbed one of Daddy's red handkerchiefs from the glove compartment and wrapped it around Cyrus's bloody stump of a finger, using a shoestring from my white sneaker as a tourniquet. I strapped Cyrus into the seat belt, put the Hyundai in gear, and slammed the accelerator to the floor, worried that if I didn't get Cyrus to the hospital fast, he might bleed to death right there in the car. I don't remember much of the trip, only Cyrus's occasional moans drowned beneath the crackle of the radio.

*   *   *

When we got to Touro, I walked Cyrus into the emergency room, and a nurse helped him onto a gurney before wheeling him through two large metal doors. I called home, but nobody answered. I sat in the waiting room for a while. After an hour or so, the doctor came out and said that Cyrus was okay. He said they'd stopped the bleeding, that Cyrus's arm was broken, that he had a cracked rib, that he'd lost a few teeth, but that he'd be okay. Even though he knew Cyrus would be okay, he said he wanted to keep him overnight for observation. He asked how Cyrus had lost his finger, and I told him I didn't know. He said Cyrus told him that he'd chopped it off in a saw while building a speaker box. I could tell by the doctor's face he knew both of us were lying.

When I got into the hospital room, Cyrus was lying in bed. He had wires stuck in his wrist, his arm was in a white cast, and his left eye was swollen closed. When he saw me, he smiled, exposing the two missing teeth.

"How are you doing?" I asked, kissing him on his forehead.

"I feel like I got the beat shit out of me," he said, a grin on his lips.

"Better watch out," I said, "before you laugh those stitches loose."

He cracked a smile. "You talk to Mama and Daddy yet?"

"I called home but nobody answered." I grabbed a pillow from the end of the bed. "Here. Put this behind your back."

Cyrus bent forward while I wedged the pillow between his back and the mattress.

"Try Daddy at the pool hall." He leaned back against the pillow, his face twisted by the pain. "You got the number?"

I reached into my purse for a pen and Cyrus called the number out to me while I wrote it down. As I was leaving, I asked Cyrus if he needed anything.

"Thanks Hailey."

I rolled my eyes.

"No. Seriously." He stared at me, each word a soft blue breath of air. "I mean it. Thank you."

When I got to the pay phone, I called the pool hall. Sure enough, Daddy was there. I didn't tell him what had happened, only that Cyrus had gone to the Emergency Room. He said he and Mama would be there soon. When I got back, Cyrus was asleep. I laid on the sofa across from Cyrus's bed and closed my eyes, listening to the rusty sound of gurneys passing through the halls until sleep rolled over me like a black wave.

Chapter Twenty-five

That night, after we got home from the hospital, Cyrus told me he was scared of what Moses might do to him if he didn't turn himself in to the police. I couldn't stand the thought of Cyrus going to jail, and I knew if he turned himself in and went to prison, there'd be no hope of saving what was left of my family. In my mind, I blamed Moses for everything.

Later, after everyone was asleep, I snuck out of the house in my nightgown and tennis shoes and climbed into Daddy's Nova. I'm not sure what I was thinking as I drove toward Moses's house. I guess part of me hoped that there was some speck of goodness left in Moses, that I could somehow plead with him, that he'd realize how important my family was to me, and that he'd agree to let Cyrus off the hook. I figured the chances were slim, but I had to at least try.

By the time I got to New Orleans East, it was almost 2 a.m. As I pulled up to Moses's trailer, I noticed his ratty green Omni parked in the grass. The porch light was on. I had to knock a few times before Moses answered, but eventually he came to the door. He didn't say a word when he opened the screen door, just smiled at me with that dirty gold tooth of his.

When I got inside, I didn't even turn around. As I stared at the picture of Jesus on the wall, I could feel Moses behind me, his words, ripe with dope, breathing down my neck. "So," he whispered, his black tarantula hand crawling along my shoulder. "You here to convince me to deliver that brother of yours from evil?"

I knew what was coming next, and I was willing to do whatever it took to convince Moses to leave my family alone, even if it meant having sex with someone as grimy as him. After all, if Meridian had taught me anything about life, it was that the way to a man's heart was through his pecker.

"I just want you to leave Cyrus alone," I said. "That's all. I'll do whatever you want. I just want you to leave him alone. My family's been through enough."

"It's like I told you before, Miss Hailey," he whispered. "Some people got to suffer before they get saved." As he said this, his hand wormed its way up the back of my nightgown and made its way to my chest, cupping my right boob. With the other hand, he grabbed a condom from the table, pulled his boxer shorts down, and slipped the condom onto his pecker. Before I knew it, he'd bent me over and pushed his pecker inside me. A soft squeal that sounded like a sack of wet puppies began to gurgle inside me, and my eyes started to fill with water. As Moses's pecker squirmed inside me, I tried to push my thoughts to the back of my head, and I started to remember this show I'd seen on the History Channel about how ancient Japanese men, to keep from getting syphilis, used condoms made out of fish bladders. I imagined some strange Japanese woman, her silk kimono cracked open, a Japanese man staring down at her through the slits of his eyes as he pushed the cold, rotten fish guts deep inside her. I could hear a strange moan crawling up Moses's throat, and when I glanced over my shoulder at him, his eyes were rolled back in his skull like the dead black eyes of a china doll. In one quick move, I pulled away from him and stumbled toward the door. When I finally got to the door, I looked back, and Moses was standing there in the dark, his sweaty skin flickering in the blue light, his pecker like a wounded black eel lowering its head.

When I got outside, I ran across the yard and back to Daddy's car, climbed in, and locked the door. As soon as I slammed the door shut,

I started crying, and soon I couldn't stop. I couldn't believe how stupid I'd been for going to Moses's house. In the back of my mind, I knew that no matter how many times I had sex with him, he'd never leave Cyrus alone. Without even thinking, I reached over, opened the glove compartment, and grabbed Daddy's loaded pistol. I unlocked the door and climbed out of the car, wiping my eyes with the back of my hand as I made my way up to Moses's front door. When I got inside, Moses was sitting on the sofa smoking a cigarette. As I got closer, I raised the pistol and Moses stood up. He stood there for a second, then took a drag off his cigarette and smiled. "Why is it every time I put my dick in some woman they somehow wind up pulling a gun on me?" Moses smiled again. "Must be my charm, I guess." He took another drag off the cigarette, blew the smoke out his nose. With the words still drifting like smoke in the air, he took a step forward, and I pulled the trigger.

The bullet ate its way into Moses's bony chest, just above his right nipple, leaving a tiny red hole that puckered like a mouth. For a moment, he looked like one of those sinners you see on TV, right when the preacher grabs them by the head and forces the demons to fly out of their skull. He opened his mouth, but nothing came out. His eyes rolled toward the floor, his finger touched the hole in his chest, and he fell to his knees. I pulled the trigger again, and the second bullet blew his head back. As he fell to the floor, I could hear his mother calling out from her room.

The minute his body hit the floor, I turned around and bolted for the door, making my way across the yard. I climbed into the car, started the engine, and pulled onto Chef Menteur Highway, the pistol like a warm hand between my legs. On the way home, just as I reached the Hwy 90 Bridge, I pulled over, put the Nova in park, and cut the engine. I climbed out of the car, and walked over to the cement guard rail. For a moment, I glanced down at the water below, then tossed the pistol over, watching the blue metal flicker against the air before it finally disappeared beneath the dead, black water.

*   *   *

After I'd gotten home, I lay in bed thinking for a while. At first, a strange sense of calm settled over me. It might sound weird, but it was almost as if, in the act of saving Cyrus, I'd somehow saved a piece of myself. I thought about how I'd spent my life waiting for God to save me and my family. Maybe I'd been wrong all along, I thought. Maybe God didn't save us after all. Maybe we had to save ourselves, and each other, first. In a twisted way, Moses had been right. When God didn't answer your prayers, you had to take matters into your own hands, and in saving Cyrus, I had done just that. But as I laid there, the sense of calm that had drifted over me started to slowly transform into fear, the way a lump of grey meat slowly turns into a fetus in a woman's stomach. I started to think about Moses, and the kid with the glass bones, and I couldn't help but wonder, if there was a God, would he forgive me for what I'd done? I began to think about the dirty little angels Chloe told me about, how they have to eat your soul before you can get into Heaven, and for a minute, as I listened to the crackle of dead leaves outside my window, I couldn't help but imagine the glorious sound of angels' teeth chewing through my tiny black soul.

--The End--

Chris Tusa was born and raised in New Orleans. He teaches in the English Department at LSU and holds an M.F.A. in Creative Writing from the University of Florida. His work has appeared in *Connecticut Review, Texas Review, Prairie Schooner, The New Delta Review, South Dakota Review, Southeast Review, Passages North,* and others. With the help of a grant from the Louisiana Div͏ he was able to complete his first book of poe͏ which was published by Louisiana Literature P͏ *Little Angels* is his first novel.